Elizabeth Was Furious.

"We were dancing," Morgan said.

"I'm sure there are a few primitives in an isolated jungle somewhere that might agree with you."

God help him, he'd missed the liquid drawl and elegant manner. Elizabeth Jeanette Beaumont played the role of lady of the manor better than anyone he'd ever met. But let others believe she was pristine through and through; he knew better. In the right hands, Liz Beaumont was hot.

Elizabeth *Kirkland*, he amended, and with a bitter twist to his lips said, "There was a time when you liked touching me."

"Times change."

"People don't, not at their core. What is can't be erased, no matter how you try to cover it up with so-called manners."

Elizabeth eyed him with a mixture of wariness and disdain. "What is that supposed to mean?"

His careless shrug was sheer acting. It helped hide the tension coiling within him. "Maybe I was just trying to get you to admit that you may have married Kirkland, but you never forgot me."

Dear Reader:

Welcome to the world of Silhouette Desire. Join me as we travel to a land of incredible passion and tantalizing romance—a place where dreams can, and do, come true.

When I read a Silhouette Desire, I sometimes feel as if I'm going on a little vacation. I can relax, put my feet up, and be transported to a new world...a world that has, naturally, a perfect hero just waiting to whisk me away! These are stories to remember, containing moments to treasure.

Silhouette Desire novels are romantic love stories—sensuous yet emotional. As a reader, you not only see the hero and heroine fall in love, you also feel what they're feeling.

Look for books by some of your favorite Silhouette Desire authors: Joan Hohl, BJ James, Linda Lael Miller and Diana Palmer.

So enjoy!

Lucia Macro
Senior Editor

HELEN R. MYERS

AFTER YOU

SILHOUETTE *Desire*

Published by Silhouette Books New York

America's Publisher of Contemporary Romance

SILHOUETTE BOOKS
300 East 42nd St., New York, N.Y. 10017

ISBN: 0-373-05599-4

First Silhouette Books printing October 1990

Printed in the U.S.A.

Books by Helen R. Myers

Silhouette Desire

Partners for Life #370
Smooth Operator #454
That Fontaine Woman! #471
The Pirate O'Keefe #506
Kiss Me Kate #570
After You #599

Silhouette Romance

Donovan's Mermaid #557
Someone to Watch over Me #643
Confidentially Yours #677
Invitation to a Wedding #737

HELEN R. MYERS

lives on a sixty-five-acre ranch deep in the piney woods of East Texas with her husband, Robert, and a constantly expanding menagerie. She lists her interests as everything that doesn't have to do with a needle and thread. When she and Robert aren't working on the house they've built together, she likes to read, garden and, of course, outfish her husband.

To My New Jersey Connection
For Nadine—who can still make me laugh
For Patrice—whose strength of character
and individuality I'd like to clone
For Patti—who introduced me
to my first romance novel
Happy Twentieth Reunion, ladies!

One

—

The majority of accidents happen within a few miles of home.

As the stench of stale water filled her nostrils, and the insurance company commercial she'd just heard on the radio echoed in her ears, Elizabeth Beaumont Kirkland barely managed to repress the wail that swelled in her lungs. But she couldn't help wondering. Did mechanical problems fit the definition of accident under some umbrella clause? And why was *she* being chosen to help keep the statistics accurate?

Then came a startling, hissing sound, followed by the woeful sight of steam spewing from beneath the hood of her Cadillac. Fully expecting flames to follow, she jerked her chrome and steel smoking dragon to the grassy shoulder of the two-lane highway.

"Not here," she moaned. "Not now!"

Killing the engine, she sat there a moment, eyeing the minigeyser before shifting her gaze to gauge the density of the storm clouds that were building overhead. They were the reason she'd been racing to get back to Meadowbrook. They were about to get a very welcome break in the unusual, mid-October heat wave that had set in over Georgia right after her sister's wedding. The impending storm promised to be ferocious, and because she was still a mile from home, the timing couldn't have been worse.

Even as she mentally calculated the distance of the storm, a bolt of lightning streaked across the low, olive-gray sky and was followed by a crack of ear-piercing thunder. Elizabeth cringed and quickly abandoned the halfhearted impulse to complete the journey on foot.

She might not be a meteorologist, but she had lived on a farm long enough to know when to pay attention to the weather. Clouds with a greenish cast usually meant hail, so even if she escaped being struck by a bolt of lightning, she would undoubtedly be pummeled by hailstones before she got near the entrance gates of the estate. It was bad enough contemplating the damage her car would suffer; there was no sense in inviting injury to herself.

Besides, she added as she glanced down at her outfit, she wasn't dressed for a cross-country sprint. Her strappy, high-heeled sandals would make it a suicidal notion, and with her luck her matching gray crepe de chine dress would probably react to water like rice paper.

Of all places for this to happen... Why did she have to end up in front of the entrance to Wildwood? For the past several weeks, specifically from the moment she had learned *who* the new owner was, she'd dreaded having to even use this road. Now she was stuck here like a sacrificial lamb. Her only consolation was that the orchard of pecan trees and the hill hid her from the view of anyone looking out from the main house. Now she needed someone to drive by— the sooner the better—and give her a ride home.

Belatedly remembering her father's and late husband's lectures about raising the hood if she ever found herself in such a predicament, she started to get out of the car. Wait a minute, came a quick afterthought, wasn't there a latch or something to release first?

Unlike her younger sister, Katherine, she knew next to nothing about cars, and, despite Kate's teasing that her ignorance was due to sheer stubbornness, she didn't plan to learn, either. It wasn't that she was incapable, and she *wasn't* prissy. She simply had a deep regard for a woman's gentility and the valuable— though increasingly fragile—role it played in modern society. She even resented the changes in the last decade or so that had made it a chore to find a service station with attendants who still pumped gas.

It was utterly ridiculous to be en route to an appointment or social function dressed in silk and pearls, only to be reduced to dodging oil puddles at a service station and, after filling up, trying to wipe the lingering scent of gas from her hands. How could men expect women to look and smell feminine, when they seemed determined to make it an impossibility?

Rounding the front of the white sedan, she did her best to wrestle her full skirt from the determined wind and frowned as steam continued to gush from the hood of the car. It no longer reminded her of a smoking dragon, but of Aladdin's lamp instead. She reached for the latch that would allow her to lift the hood completely. Wouldn't a genie come in handy now? she brooded. One with a degree in mechanical engineering, so he could fix whatever was wrong and get her out of here.

"Ouch!"

She lifted her burned fingers to her lips and blew. That did it. Someone was going to hear about this. The car was barely a year old and had been serviced only last month! Her father had always been conscientious about making sure his daughters drove in well-tended vehicles, and since her move back to Meadowbrook, he'd matter-of-factly resumed that responsibility.

Obviously someone had forgotten to check something. What was the problem? The radiator? A pump of some kind? She had to admit it was frustrating not to have the slightest idea. More frustrating was the realization that another car had yet to pass. She glanced up and down the empty road. Granted, this wasn't exactly the interstate, but she was less than thirty miles from Atlanta!

She took a deep, calming breath. If the worse came to worst, she would wait out the storm in her car. The one thing she *wasn't* going to do was go up to ask Morgan for help or the use of his phone. Taking her chances with the lightning and hail would be preferable to being near him again.

As she assured herself of that, a pickup came around the bend. Relief and gratitude melted the frown marring her brow, and she curved her lips into a welcoming smile. Seconds later she recognized the gleaming black truck...the driver...and that what she'd been dreading most was about to come true.

"Please, no," she whispered, feeling the blood drain from her face and maybe even her heart.

She watched with macabre fascination as he slowed, pulled in behind her car and shut off the engine. Then he simply sat there staring at her. Even from a car length away, one look from those onyx eyes forced her to lock her knees in order to keep them from buckling. "Cobra eyes" were what she'd heard her new brother-in-law call them upon *their* initial meeting. It was an apt description. No one had ever been able to read Morgan Deveroux's eyes when he didn't want them to, and as a rule he didn't.

The wind intensified, blowing her hair into her eyes, playing havoc with her skirt. With one hand she combed back the annoying curls, and with the other she tried to lower her dress before it could billow to an indecent level. Knowing Morgan, he would look his fill, then accuse her of intentionally stirring up the wind. It wasn't an exaggeration; after all, he had accused her of more bizarre things.

"Come on," she muttered through stiff lips. "Get it over with."

But he took his time getting out of the truck and paused to glance up at the sky as a few, huge drops of rain began to fall. Elizabeth watched his chest rise and fall with a heavy sigh, the action threatening to undo the top two buttons on his denim work shirt. It triggered memories of other times and places, of how he'd looked without a shirt, while pitching fresh hay into the horse stalls at Meadowbrook.

The coal-black mat of hair covering his powerful chest would glisten like anthracite from the sweat that collected there. When he breathed deeply, his well-formed shoulders, back and arms would gleam like polished marble, leaving her heart pounding and her throat incredibly dry. He was only slightly above average height, but he was magnificent, built with a solidness that commanded respect and attracted stares.

His face was equally compelling and memorable. Maybe it was his hard, squared features or the gypsy-dark coloring that gave him the look of a rogue. At any rate, he did nothing to temper the impression, not even keeping his thick, wavy hair trimmed so that he would look more—civilized. He still wore it long, so that it tended to sweep down over his broad forehead and brush against his collar. But she had to concede that a haircut alone wouldn't make him look any less predatory, because there would still be those eyes—those unwavering, unforgiving eyes. Even now, when she was hardly the naive child she had been, Elizabeth found it difficult to meet his steady gaze. As he finally approached her, hard-won self-discipline alone kept her from taking a cautionary step backward. It helped to remember one of her father's favorite maxims: there *were* moments when face was more important than self-preservation.

If he noticed her unease, he ignored it. Reaching into the back pocket of his jeans, he drew out a rag and, using it to protect his fingers, unlatched and raised the hood. For a moment he was enveloped by a cloud of steam.

Elizabeth stared, feeling as if she were caught up in some surrealistic play. With a quick shake of her head, she shifted to peer around his shoulder. "What do you think the problem is?"

At first she thought he was going to ignore her and, suppressing a surge of annoyance, began repeating the question. But the droplets of rain grew in number, temporarily distracting her. She glanced down at her dress and bit her lower lip.

"Get in the car."

She might have—if he hadn't *ordered* her or used that obnoxiously bossy tone of voice. The dress was an original, and, contrary to what was written in the social columns, she did her best to make her clothes last several seasons. But hearing that autocratic intonation, the same one he had used when she'd been sixteen years old, had her placing her hands on her hips and lifting her chin.

"Now see here, Morgan Deveroux," she began, determined to give him a piece of her mind, once and for all.

"Will you get in the car, woman! Can't you tell that all hell's about to break—?"

Before he could finish, the heavens opened in a blinding deluge; within seconds Elizabeth found herself as drenched as if she'd walked off the dock and into the pond behind the house. To heck with principle, she decided, and raced for cover.

She jumped into the car, only mildly conscious of—even grateful for—the white leather seats that wouldn't be damaged by the water sluicing off her. About to reach for her purse to get the packet of tissues she always carried, she was startled by Morgan appearing at the passenger door. He tried to open it. Naturally it was locked. She might not have the sense to avoid getting soaked, but she did practice caution when driving alone.

He pounded his fist against the window with a force that threatened to shatter it. "Damn it—open up!"

Acting on reflex, she did—only to recoil a moment later, backing up until she was flat against the driver's door as he more than filled his side of the front seat. Don't be a silly goose, she quickly chastised herself. Intimidating or not, *no one* had the right to snarl at her like a bad-tempered, junkyard dog.

"If you insist on waiting out the storm in my car, would you at least have the courtesy to do so without cursing me?" she asked archly.

Morgan paused midway in slicking his hair back off his forehead and gave her an incredulous look. Rivulets of water coursed an erratic path down his angular face. "Insist? What did you expect me to do, stay out there and drown?"

The question was too ridiculous to warrant a reply. He might despise her, but he should remember that she often went to extreme lengths to avoid hurting people. With a look that said as much, she returned to the task of hunting for the tissues. When she found them, she drew out two and, unable to abandon etiquette entirely, offered the packet to him.

"What do you expect me to do with that bit of fluff?"

How like him to make a mockery of the gesture. Once she would have tried to explain that she'd only meant to help. Now, though his rejection still had the ability to sting, she knew better than to rise to the bait he dangled. Silently listing one or two things she would like to suggest he try, she tossed the packet onto the dashboard and concentrated on dabbing what moisture she could from her own face.

No, he hadn't changed. If anything, he was more insufferable than ever.

Fourteen years ago he'd been the twenty-year-old drifter her father, in one of his innumerable softhearted moments, had hired as a temporary stable hand. To his credit, Morgan had worked hard, soon exhibiting such an impressive gift for handling horses that the job became a permanent one. What they would belatedly discover was that he also possessed an infuriating knack of aggravating people. Elizabeth was convinced she had been his choice victim.

She'd been sixteen—a serious sixteen, since her mother had died early on and, as her father's older daughter, it became her responsibility to supervise the domestic side of running Meadowbrook. Morgan teased her endlessly about that and called her names such as Queen Liz or your ladyship. What was even more frustrating, he undermined any attempt she made to keep her younger sister, Kate, from turning into a tomboy.

But Elizabeth had also been attracted to his dark looks, intrigued by his mysterious past and mesmerized by his intense nature. Her maturity did not extend to having much experience in matters regarding the opposite sex, but she knew enough to recognize that with him she was way out of her depth. Unfortunately it hadn't made much difference. Something volatile and not quite civilized simmered between them, and for four years she had struggled with a growing temptation to test it.

She was no longer that painfully naive teenager. In what she still believed had been her eleventh hour, she'd come to her senses and made a decision that removed her from temptation permanently. Now thirty, she was older and wiser. Cured, she insisted with a mental nod of satisfaction. There was no denying that the man remained an enigma to her, and probably always would, but that reckless urge to match wills with him, to see how far she could test her rein on passion was gone. Passion alone hadn't been enough for her. It certainly hadn't been enough to make her turn her back on responsibility—to herself and to her family. And Morgan . . . as always, he'd survived.

He'd left Meadowbrook the night her father announced her engagement to Daniel Kirkland. He'd left Georgia entirely, going who knew where, but he'd become successful. Wildwood was his now, and he was establishing his own breeding farm. How he'd managed it and why he'd chosen to come back here were questions that kept coming up, no matter where she went these days. If she'd had a say in the matter, he would have stayed away. Though they'd only come face-to-face once since his return—and then only because her exasperating sister had insisted on inviting him to her wedding—the experience had been enough to convince Elizabeth that she would be better off avoiding him.

But how did one avoid a man who was taking up two-thirds of the front seat of one's car?

Reassuring herself that she could be civil to practically anyone for a few minutes, she tentatively glanced back at him—only to experience the same panicky feeling she'd had when finding herself suddenly dancing with him at Kate and Giles's reception.

Like hers, his clothes were plastered to his body. One powerful, jean-clad thigh was a twitch away from hers. With every breath she took, she was reminded of his musky, male scent and of the time he'd crushed her close, vowing she would take him to her pristine bed, if only as a ghost in her dreams.

He had always been that sure of himself. At the wedding last week his behavior had been beyond confident; clearly he'd been intent on proving she was still vulnerable to him. He'd almost succeeded—though she was adamant that it was more surprise than latent feelings that had made her tremble when he drew her into his arms on the dance floor. She wasn't the inexperienced teenager she'd once been, and focusing solely on her car trouble would prove it to him.

"You haven't told me what you think the problem is."

Morgan almost laughed, though the sound wouldn't have reflected the slightest hint of humor. "The problem," as she so delicately put it, was that sitting beside her like this made him feel as though he were being stretched on a rack.

As usual, he'd waited too long before paying attention to his physical and—damned if he would apologize for it—thoroughly natural needs. Work, as always, came first. Consequently he had a great deal of—energy stored up, and had yet to take the time to expend it.

The last thing he had anticipated or needed when he came around the bend was to find *her* literally parked outside his front gate. He knew better than to consider her a gift from the gods; more likely she was simply another knife in the ribs from the devil himself.

She'd stood there in front of Detroit's version of a white charger, looking very much like a folklore heroine with her golden-blond curls and that filmy dress, which even when dry had sent his temperature soaring. Now, soaked and clinging to her slender but tantalizing curves, it reminded him of things he would rather forget, such as how he'd been bewitched by her from the beginning and how, despite all the years and his determination, he wasn't free yet. He had a truckload of feed that, though covered with plastic, was in danger of getting drenched and thus ruined. But all he could think about was that she still got to him.

"A clamp broke, and the water hose slipped free," he muttered, turning his head to look out the passenger window. The wind was really whipping now, tearing at the leaves and nuts on the pecan trees, ripping many free and torturing the most flexible limbs into unnatural angles. He wholeheartedly sympathized with their plight. "You might consider having this thing serviced once in a while, when you're not too busy attending your tea and crumpet parties."

She began to tell him she hadn't been attending any "tea and crumpet" party and that the car had just been in the shop, but bit back the response when she realized it was undoubtedly what he wanted. Instead she squeezed the excess moisture out of her hair so that it would stop trickling down her neck and tickling her. Murder, she must look like a wet poodle with this newly permed hair.

"I'm sorry if I'm keeping you from something important," she said with formal politeness.

"Just work."

It wasn't the most encouraging of answers, but at least he hadn't snarled. Dropping the soaked tissues onto the floor mat, she removed the silver earrings that suddenly seemed to weigh twice as much as when she'd first put them on. She dropped them into her purse.

"Is it going well? The work at Wildwood, I mean. Are you about settled in?"

"Why the sudden interest? Running out of things to gossip about at your social gatherings?" He watched with satisfaction as the nostrils of her perfect, patrician nose flared with her indrawn breath. There had always been something regal about her face, her entire bearing. Once it had eased some of his inner torment to remind her that she was merely mortal like the rest of the human race. It seemed old habits were slow to die, though now the indulgence primarily left him feeling like a fool.

"I'd have thought that by now, as a businessman, you'd have cultured some social graces. Or am I wrong in guessing you treat everyone with the same lack of civility that you treat me?"

"Was that civility you exhibited at Kate's wedding?"

A particularly bright flash of lightning, followed by a dense clap of thunder, gave Elizabeth the seconds she needed to collect herself. No, she hadn't behaved her best toward him; but then he hadn't exactly been the soul of propriety himself. "When a man forces himself on a woman, she needn't be burdened with the social responsibility of remaining a lady."

"We were dancing."

"I'm sure there are a few primitives in an isolated jungle somewhere that might agree with you."

God help him, he'd missed that liquid drawl and elegant syntax. Elizabeth Jeanette Beaumont played the role of ice queen or lady of the manor better than anyone he had ever met. But let others believe she was pristine through and through; he knew better. In the right hands, Liz Beaumont was hot.

Elizabeth *Kirkland*, he amended, and said with a bitter twist to his lips, "There was a time when you liked touching me."

"Times change." She shifted to slip out of one shoe and wipe the moisture and sand from her nylon-clad foot.

Morgan lifted his gaze from delectable toes and delicate ankle to the view the dropped bodice of her dress provided. His mouth went dry and felt as rough as heavy-duty sandpaper. Heat collected in his loins. He didn't need to be reminded of how beautifully she was formed. He had haunted dreams—and a few memories—to do that for him.

"People don't, not at their core. What is can't be erased, no matter how you try to cover it up with so-called manners."

Elizabeth brushed her hair back from her face and eyed him with a mixture of wariness and disdain. "What is that supposed to mean?"

His careless shrug was sheer acting. It helped hide the tension coiling within him. "Maybe I was just trying to get you to admit that you may have married Kirkland, but you never forgot me."

She could feel her face flood with the heat of embarrassment. Of all the arrogant— "How could I forget the man who enjoyed dragging everyone down to his level?"

"My 'level' used to turn you on."

"Marriage refined my slipping tastes."

Morgan's laugh was brief and hard. "Sex between you two must have been as exciting as watching mold grow."

"Daniel and I called it making *love*."

He'd asked for that, but it still cut deeply and made the simmering anger he'd been harboring for all these years intensify. "Yeah? And what do you call what you're wearing, the latest in widow's weeds?"

"It's been a year." Elizabeth ground out the words, refusing to look at him.

"What's a year, when you look so good in black?"

She shut her eyes tightly, determined he wouldn't see the tears that suddenly burned there. "If you don't mind, I would prefer not to discuss my husband or my marriage with you."

Morgan stared at her soft, full mouth for a moment before giving himself a mental shake. "I'm surprised you moved back to Meadowbrook. I would have thought the place Kirkland bought for you would be hard to give up."

How like him to be so persistent, Elizabeth thought with an inward sigh. Well, he might not offer her his condolences for her loss, but he had no right to mock her for being close to her family. "Meadowbrook is too big for one person, and my father is terribly lonely there. Daniel's death made me more sensitive to that."

What she wanted, Morgan thought uncharitably as he eyed the wedding ring she had yet to remove, was the best of both worlds. She had returned to being Teddy Beaumont's protected and pampered daughter, playing hostess for all his business and social functions, and she still reaped the sympathy that went along with being the bereaved widow. Of course, considering the size of the diamonds in her ring, he could understand her reluctance to lock it away in a safe. Why should she, when it was a perfect accompaniment to her pale, blond beauty?

"Why did *you* move back?" she asked, determined to direct their conversation away from herself.

"Impulse."

"Why next door?"

"It was for sale.... The price was right." He shrugged and cast her a sly glance. "Why? Worried that I might want to renew old friendships?"

Feeling her heart give a nervous skip, Elizabeth bent again to remove her other shoe. "We were never friends, Morgan."

"What would you have called it?" he drawled, following the move and once again drinking his fill of the view. "We never quite made it to lovers—though it wasn't for lack of opportunity."

Elizabeth crushed the already clumped tissues in her fist and gave him a withering look. "You, sir, are no gentleman."

"And you can't exactly have called us enemies," he continued, ignoring her. "Even though I think you enjoyed riling me . . . seeing how far you could push."

"Look who's talking. You're the one who always criticized me. I could never ride. I didn't know how to dress. My friends were either shallow or freeloading social climbers." She ticked off the list on her fingers. "You thrived on pointing out my shortcomings to me whenever the opportunity arose."

"I liked seeing you get steamed. You were always at your best when your claws were bared and your eyes were gleaming like a cat intent on drawing blood."

"You were despicable then, and you still are."

A storm might be raging outside, but Elizabeth, her blood pounding at her temples, her hands shaking with fury, decided it was preferable to spending another minute in the same car with *him*. Tossing away the tissues, she bent to put her shoes back on.

"Hell, can't you stop squirming for five seconds?" Morgan muttered, discovering too late that much as he'd enjoyed riling her, he'd also succeeded in getting himself aroused, as well. "At the rate you're going, you'll wear out that leather before the damned car warranty expires."

"Oh!" Elizabeth jerked upright, her eyes flashed. "I don't know why I ever bothered trying to understand you or help you, Morgan Deveroux."

"Help me what?" he shot back. "Be like those so-called friends of yours, the ones you always abandoned if it meant you could spend five minutes with me?"

"How could I have ever believed that there was an ounce of decency in you? You're rude, crude and—"

"And I made you feel things no one else could," he said softly, smoothly, narrowing his eyes as he dropped them to her breasts. "I still can—or are you going to deny that your body is already excited?"

"That's fury!"

He reached out and brushed the backs of his fingers over a distended nipple clearly outlined by the soaked, sheer dress. "That's arousal, sweetheart. What's the matter? Did living with that *gentleman* husband of yours fog up your memory of what the real thing feels like?"

She swung out, intent on slapping him, but he was faster, stronger. One moment her wrist was enclosed in a crushing grip; the next she was being dragged across the seat.

"Morgan—don't!" she whispered shakily, at once terrified of the heat devouring the oxygen in the car, terrified of the intent she saw in his eyes.

He hesitated for a fraction of a moment, absorbing the tension in her. Shock and fear shone in her exquisite, blue-gray eyes. When next he looked into them, he promised himself, he would see desire. Then he would walk away from her.

With the promise a bitter taste in his mouth, he locked his lips to hers.

For ten years he'd been storing up the anger. She'd rejected him. He had given her more of himself than he'd ever given to another soul, and she'd rejected him, gone into the arms of another man. She had to pay for that. He wanted to show her that he'd survived and that he no longer cared. Only first she should understand what it felt like to be used and then rejected.

But the moment the kiss began, the instant he took possession, all thinking stopped. It was enough to taste that moist sweetness again, to draw it deep and bathe his senses in it. It didn't matter that she was resisting him, that she continued to hold herself rigid in his arms, that she was still trying to evade the caress of his tongue over hers. The pleasure was already acute, and he wanted to prolong it. He had so much hunger to assuage.

This couldn't be happening, Elizabeth thought, successfully wrenching her mouth from his and gulping down some much-needed oxygen. He couldn't be doing this. What was worse, she couldn't want it. But the fogged-up windows, the steamy, stifling heat they were producing, underscored the obvious: at least in one respect nothing had changed. He still possessed a power over her. With a minimum of effort he could still reduce her to a mindless, wanton creature.

"Morgan, if there's an ounce of mercy in you—"

"None," he muttered, an instant before he committed the same erotic assault on the delicate shell of her ear.

Elizabeth bit back the moan that rose to her lips, but there was nothing she could do to hide her shiver of response to the sensual attack. She told herself that she despised him for this, but physically she wanted, *needed* it. Already her breasts were swollen and throbbing. Her womb ached with an indescribable emptiness.

She wasn't aware of surrendering; but one moment she relaxed the fists that had been pushing against his granite-hard chest, and the next she was clutching handfuls of his shirt. Then, blindly seeking his mouth with hers, she allowed her body the intimate contact it craved.

Fever. Morgan groaned as it scorched him. Yet he met her passion with equal fervor. Kissing her had always been like this—almost as satisfying as the ultimate act itself. Almost enough, yet not enough. He wanted more. Everything.

The realization had him reeling. Fiercely gripping her waist, he pushed her to a safer arm's distance. Lord, what a fool he'd been. What made him think he could punish her with kisses? He stared at her smoky, dazed eyes and her kiss-soft lips and cursed himself for his stupidity and weakness. All he'd succeeded in doing was proving to himself that nothing had changed, except that his desire for her had intensified.

Disgusted, he reached over and wrenched the keys out of the ignition. Then, snatching up her purse, he flung open the car door and all but dragged her out into the pouring rain.

"Stop it!" she cried, still caught in an emotional and physical vertigo. The grass was slick, the rain blinding and she clutched at his shirt with her free hand to keep from falling. "Morgan, what are you doing?"

"Coming to my senses," he said, hauling her toward his truck. It might be impossible to cure himself, but he sure as hell could salvage what was left.

Cursing the day he'd ever met her, Morgan drove her home.

Two

A mile equaled one silent scream, the full recital of the beatitudes, ten fingernail grooves in a favorite and outrageously expensive suede purse, and an aching jaw from clenching her teeth together. But a mile wasn't nearly far enough to diffuse, let alone conquer, Elizabeth's anger.

Morgan had barely brought the truck to a halt before her family's stately, white-pillared mansion when she bolted for freedom, The vehicle actually shook as she slammed the door behind her. It gave her so much satisfaction she tried it again with the heavy front door, though from the sound of squealing tires she knew the effect was lost on Morgan.

Well, she hadn't done it for his benefit, anyway, Elizabeth assured herself as she dabbed a drop of water from the tip of her nose. When she spotted both Leona and her father watching her from opposite

doorways, however, she took one look at their aston-
ished faces and decided she would be pushing it if she
gave in to the impulse to fling her purse at her reflec-
tion in the ornate foyer mirror.

"Lord have mercy..." Leona whispered, pressing
a work-roughened hand to her bosom.

"Hell's bells," Theodore Beaumont muttered, lifting his heavy eyebrows to a point where they nearly
merged with his steel-gray hair.

No, Elizabeth thought, there were some things they
simply wouldn't be able to adjust to, and she wasn't
going to shock them any more than they already were.
Kate was the vociferous one in the family, the one who
could tear through the house with the fury of a virago
or the glee of an exuberant child. No one expected her
to hide her feelings, because Kate was Kate.

She, on the other hand, was reliable, sensible Elizabeth, the sedate one with an unswerving respect for
proper decorum. She was also the one who struggled
never to disappoint, rarely complained, and *didn't* allow her emotions to get the better of her. But for a few
moments that infuriating man had almost made her
forget all that.

"Hello...Dad...Leona..." With her arms akimbo,
she offered a weak smile in apology for the puddle she
was creating on the painstakingly polished hardwood
floor. "It's raining."

"Either that or you came home by way of the duck
pond," Leona replied, recovering from her tongue-
tied state and shifting her hands to her ample hips.
"What on earth happened?"

"I had car trouble."

"I knew it," Teddy declared, thrusting out his
chest, though his belly still won by inches. He poked

a beefy finger at her. "How many times have I told you girls that you should let Clarence drive you when you need to go somewhere?"

"Dad, I talked to you about getting a ride on Monday, but by the time I came downstairs this morning to remind you, you'd already left in the limousine."

"Oh. I—er—had an early appointment," he said, giving her a look of chagrin. "All right, enough about that. Just tell me that you're not hurt or anything."

"I'm fine. But you're going to have to call for a service truck to go get the car."

"Get it from where?"

"I told you that wasn't her using the driveway like it was a drag strip," Leona said, giving the elder Beaumont a knowing nod.

Leona had served as the family's housekeeper for more than twenty years, and the lines separating employee and employer had grown comfortably faint. Elizabeth could only guess what kind of lively exchange Leona and her father had shared before she came in. But there were more pressing things to think about. She cast her father a wary glance. "No—it wasn't me. It was Morgan Deveroux."

Teddy's eyes widened and his coloring deepened, as though he'd taken a sharp elbow in his midsection. "Deveroux? That rogue? Didn't I make it clear at your sister's wedding that the years had done nothing to change my opinion of that scoundrel and that I didn't want you anywhere near him? It's bad enough that Kate disregards my feelings, but—"

"I didn't disobey you, Dad. It simply happened that I was in front of Wildwood when steam started pouring out of the car. Not knowing what to expect, I pulled over, hoping that someone would stop and help.

That someone turned out to be Morgan and—do you think I could have a brandy?''

It was so unlike her to ask for anything other than wine or sherry that Teddy and his housekeeper exchanged concerned looks. ''Better get some towels, Leona, and give old Quisenberry a call,'' he instructed. ''She might have caught a chill.''

''I'm fine,'' Elizabeth insisted. But after glancing down at the expanding puddle at her feet, she grimaced. ''Let me go upstairs and get out of these wet things. When I come down you can change that drink to a sherry, all right?''

Without waiting for a reply, she hurried up the double-width staircase. It was true enough that she needed to change, but after Morgan's harsh words of criticism, she also needed a few moments alone to collect herself—and to decide how much of what had happened she was going to share with her father. He'd never known about Morgan and herself. Back then he'd been busy enough with his business and trying to keep up with Kate's misadventures.... Elizabeth hadn't wanted to upset him with news of her bickering with Morgan. She certainly didn't want him to know about the rest.

Once inside her room, she leaned back against the door and closed her eyes tightly. She could still feel the impact of Morgan's kisses racing through her bloodstream. Her body felt weak and disturbingly naked, now that it no longer had his to warm her. *It's because you still can't get used to sleeping alone at night,* she told herself, grasping for an acceptable explanation. *It's because you still miss Daniel.*

That's what it must be.

That's all she would let it be.

Taking a deep breath, she opened her eyes and looked around the room she'd grown up in. She had redecorated it since moving back, partly because she needed to keep herself occupied, partly because it had held too many memories that were best forgotten.

It was quietly elegant, a place where she liked to come to read or simply think. She credited that to the soothing shade of hunter green that she'd picked up from the background of the floral wallpaper and used again in the carpeting. The bedding, an ecru lace-on-white-linen spread and two matching pillow covers, had come from one of her mother's chests in the attic. When she was suffering from insomnia, it was soothing to trace the patterns of the lace with her fingertips. The detailed work reminded her of how her mother, even while lying ill in bed, had tried to work on her crocheting every day. Doilies. Small things, because, as Elizabeth would later understand, she'd been concerned with finishing what she'd started.

The feminine writing desk by the window had been her mother's, as well, and it was Elizabeth's favorite possession. She hadn't inherited her mother's skill with a crochet hook, but did possess her fondness for corresponding. It was a rare day when Elizabeth didn't spend at least an hour sitting there with a cup of tea, writing an epistle to a friend or relative. Or writing in her personal journal, she thought, eyeing the desk longingly. How nice it would be to do so now. Perhaps she might even reconcile a few things in her own mind. But her father was waiting downstairs. If she didn't hurry, he would start bellowing for her from the foot of the staircase.

When she stepped into the study, she found the self-made millionaire taking a call and doing what he obviously enjoyed best—negotiating tough business terms for some deal or other. After signaling that she was content to wait, Elizabeth took a seat in one of the Italian leather chairs that faced his desk.

She often shared a predinner drink with her father in this room. It was masculine but unpretentious with its warm-toned oak paneling, red leather chairs and blue and red-patterned, hooked rugs. Kate jokingly referred to it as the "war counsel" room, but like Elizabeth she, too, had spent her share of time as a child curled up behind the heavy, indigo-blue draperies on the tall windows. They would entertain themselves with books from their father's extensive library while waiting for him to finish his business and take them for a ride or to the city for lunch. The best times were in the winter, when the sun warmed the room from the outside and a lively, crackling fire warmed it from within.

No sunshine beamed in through the windows this afternoon, and, though it appeared the storm was diminishing, the sky remained gray and the rolling thunder lingered.

Teddy hung up the phone, his frown deepening as he considered her attire. "Are you sure you're feeling okay?"

Elizabeth smoothed the skirt of her butter-colored, cashmere robe. "Don't start reading things into this. I know I rarely come downstairs unless I'm completely dressed, but I thought I would take a hot bath after that sherry."

He eyed her for another moment before rubbing his hand along his whisker-rough jaw. Then pushing himself out of his chair, he crossed over to the bar cart. "That was Clifton Ambrose's agent on the phone just now. Ambrose is interested in coming down from New York to direct the theater's first season.''

''That's wonderful,'' Elizabeth replied, though she had to dig to muster any real enthusiasm. Normally it would be there. She loved the theater, and getting the famed director to come to Georgia for even one show would be a coup. But fatigue—no, stress—was taking its toll. She forced herself to focus on her father's latest project and what this could mean. Beaumont Center was going to be the newest business-and-entertainment center in Atlanta, but at the moment it was hardly more than cement and steel girders. ''Do you think the center will be finished on schedule?''

''Giles assures me he would have postponed his and Kate's honeymoon if his people didn't have things under control. I trust his judgment.'' Having poured two drinks, he carried them across the room and, handing her one, sat down in the matching chair beside hers. He watched her settle the wineglass in her lap and took a long sip of his brandy. ''I already phoned Clarence about your car. As soon as the storm passes, he'll go see what needs to be done.''

''Thank you,'' she murmured, wishing they could forget the matter entirely. ''Did Kate call?''

''Sweetheart, she's on her honeymoon.''

''I called when I was on my honeymoon.''

His expression softened. ''So you did.'' The grandfather clock in the foyer chimed the quarter hour, snapping him out of his momentary reminiscing. ''Er, about this function you attended today...I'm afraid I don't recall—''

''Dad, you needn't apologize. You're a busy man. You can't expect to remember everything. It was the civic luncheon to honor women in service fields. I was

chosen to present an award to the off-duty nurse
who'd saved the pregnant woman trapped in that
burning car this past spring.''

''I remember now. Well, good for you. I'm glad to
see you keeping yourself busy. Was she pleased?''

''No, I think she was embarrassed. After the cere-
mony she told me she didn't feel comfortable being
rewarded for doing what she felt was the right thing.
It was quite humbling to listen to her. It made me
think about my own life and what little I'm doing with
it.''

''The devil, you say. Why, you have one of the most
hectic social schedules of anyone I know.''

''Isn't that the truth,'' Elizabeth replied dryly. ''I'm
beginning to think Kate was right when she said that
if a week goes by and my picture hasn't made the society pages of the newspaper, people begin wondering
if I've been shepherded to Switzerland for a tummy
tuck or to one of those discreet, dependency rehabilitation places.''

''What are you saying?''

The surprise in his voice, the touch of distress in his
eyes made her hesitate to explain. She understood
what was behind his reaction. Teddy Beaumont was
one of the most devoted fathers a daughter could wish
for. He bragged about his girls, pampered and protected them with equal parts of peacock, Santa Claus
and grizzly bear. But when it came to comprehending
what made them tick, what went on in any woman's
head, he was mystified.

''Never mind. I suppose it's nothing more than fatigue talking. I didn't sleep well last night,'' she admitted, knowing there was no way he could miss the
faint shadows under her eyes, since the rain had all but

washed away her make-up. Slightly self-conscious, she raised her glass to her lips.

"Elizabeth, my dear...Quisenberry told you the first anniversary would be the hardest. I know it was for me when your mother passed away," he added gruffly.

She remembered. But what Dr. Quisenberry hadn't told her was that she would lie awake nights, feeling as angry as she was heartsick. And worst of all, she didn't have the vaguest notion of how to deal with that.

It filled her with shame. Daniel had been on his way home from one of his business trips when his commuter flight went down in bad weather. He'd been such a bright man, a warm, caring man with everything to look forward to. He'd deserved better. *They* had deserved better.

Yes, she was angry. Fate had robbed her of more than a good friend and husband; it had robbed her of children—at least the flicker of hope that she still might conceive. It had robbed her of her sense of worth, even of a reason to get up in the morning. Perhaps their marriage hadn't been the exalted union poets write of, but she hadn't asked for fairy tales or even excitement. She had accepted Daniel's proposal—quietly, calmly accepted him, because she *knew* they were suited to each other. She'd made him happy. She'd made her father happy. Why had she been punished?

"Let me call him for you," Teddy said, breaking into her thoughts. "He can prescribe a mild sedative for you."

Sedative? Elizabeth shook her head. "No, Dad. I'll be all right. It's been a long day, that's all."

Teddy didn't look convinced. "Princess, would you mind telling me what caused you to burst into the house like that? It had to be something that Deveroux said to you."

"But nothing worth repeating," she insisted. She knew she had to tell him something, but she needed to be careful not to give away too much. "Dad, you were never aware of this, but Morgan and I . . . never got along. Oh, I tried not to let it show when you were around, but—"

"Elizabeth, *no one* got along with Morgan all the time."

"Well, suffice it to say he still believes I was cut from a different cloth than you and Kate, and this afternoon he merely pointed out that he had little use for 'my kind.' "

"Your 'kind'?"

"His reference to the 'idle rich.' Anyway, when you think about it, these days the label almost fits."

"I won't have you talking about yourself like that," Teddy declared, his voice rumbling like the thunder. "And I won't stand for him speaking to you that way, either. Confound the man! Maybe he did have some tough breaks as a boy, but hell, is that an excuse for going through life with a chip on his shoulder?"

Elizabeth couldn't quite hide her surprise or curiosity. "You never said you knew about Morgan's past. Whenever I asked him about it, he'd make some sarcastic comment or else never reply at all."

"Can't say I do know much. He never admitted or denied having a family. But Jackson once told me that every payday he would catch a ride to the city, and when he'd come back the next day, he'd be broke and in a foul temper. I never saw him abuse liquor, so all I can figure is that he was meeting someone there." Teddy cleared his throat. "Of course, he could have had a weakness of another kind."

What other kind? Elizabeth wondered, gripping the stem of her glass. Women? That was almost laughable, because anyone with eyes could see that even now Morgan Deveroux wouldn't have to *pay* for a woman.

What did that leave? Drinking? She couldn't remember ever seeing him drink anything alcoholic. Gambling?

"He understood the horses, I'll give him that," Teddy continued as if reminiscing himself. "Every bit as good as Jackson. But it doesn't excuse the way he walked out on me. I tolerated a lot, putting up with his sass and his stubborn ways. The least he could have done was to give me notice before leaving. Remember? Jackson was still in the hospital recovering from that gallbladder operation, so we were shorthanded, anyway—"

"I remember, Dad. It was the weekend Daniel and I became engaged."

Teddy brightened. "Well, so it was. Ach, the years seem to be slipping by faster and faster. At any rate, there was no call for him to up and skip town like that, and I'm not about to let him forget it. Just because the man's turned his luck around—and you know under normal circumstances I'd be the first to congratulate him for that—doesn't mean he's wiped the slate clean. Why, he didn't even come over and pay his respects when he moved in next door. I have a good mind to go over there and set him straight on a few things, here and now."

"No!" Elizabeth cried, almost spilling her wine. That was the last thing she needed. "Let's forget it, Dad. Like it or not, he's our neighbor, and it won't do to start feuding like a couple of backwoods clans."

At first Teddy looked determined, but after studying her pale face for a moment, he reluctantly nodded. "All right. But you can't blame me for wanting to take care of my own."

"I love you for it." Rising, she leaned over to give him an affectionate kiss on the cheek. "Now if you'll excuse me, I think I'll take this upstairs and have that bath. See you at dinner?"

"Wouldn't miss it, Princess. But I'd prefer you try to lie down and take a nap. Leona won't mind holding dinner."

Elizabeth smiled and assured him that she would think about it, but as she climbed the stairs back to her room, she knew sleep was out of the question. How could she find comfort in sleep, when a phantom haunted her dreams—a taunting phantom with onyx eyes?

Morgan considered it a miracle his driving didn't land him in a ditch, but he made it back to Wildwood with nothing more than a few pounds of mud splattering the rear of the truck. It still left him with his fury, but he found an outlet for that the moment he pulled up to the stables and saw his prize stallion, clearly just in from a workout, abandoned without a proper cooling and grooming.

Oblivious to the drizzle still falling and the feed in the bed of the truck, he braked sharply and shifted into Park. "Sawyer!" he roared, jumping out and causing Dancer's Prize to jerk at his crossties.

The sound of the back door of the main house being slammed had Morgan spinning around, and he watched a squat, middle-aged man scurry awkwardly toward him. One hand held down his weatherworn fedora, the other clutched his thigh and served as a brace for his stiff left leg. Morgan had met Spud Mahoney ten years ago, only weeks after leaving Meadowbrook, and they'd been together ever since. But there was nothing nostalgic in Morgan's tone when the man got within hearing distance.

"Damn it, Mahoney, can't I leave this place for an hour without everything going to hell? Where's Sawyer?"

"Now hold on, Morgan, you'll upset Dancer."

"He already is upset. That worthless kid—" Morgan slapped his fist against the side of his truck. "Any *novice* knows not to let a horse cool down too rapidly. And where the devil were you to let this happen?"

"Playing secretary, because your phone's been ringing ever since you left!" Spud shouted back with equal fervor. But it was wasted, since Morgan was already on his way to check on the stallion. "I knew the kid was out working him," he called after him, "but I thought he was long back by the time the storm started. I meant to check as soon as I got off the phone."

Morgan gripped Dancer's reins and ran his other hand soothingly down the horse's neck. Then he checked for body temperature by touching the chestnut stallion between his front legs. With a curse that sounded more like a hiss, Morgan freed Dancer from where he'd been temporarily tied and began walking him around the stable. "It'll be a miracle if all he does

is get cramps. I swear, Spud, if he's caught a chill,
I'll—''

"Hey, Morgan. You back already?''

Without a word, Morgan shoved Dancer's reins into
Spud's hands. Then, wheeling around, he grabbed the
younger man by the front of his T-shirt and thrust him
against a stable wall. "Give me a good reason not to
knock you straight into next week.''

"C'mon, man. What did I do?''

"Guess.''

Eddie, reaching for the ground with his feet, glanced
from the horse to his employer. His Adam's apple
bobbled as he swallowed. "Uh—I was only gone a
second. I swear it. I had to change. We got caught in
the storm. Do you want your best rider to catch pneu-
monia?''

"Better the rider than the horse.''

Eddie risked a sarcastic grunt. "Yeah, I believe it.
Well, I'm here now, okay?''

"I have potential clients coming tomorrow, lining
up studs for their mares for next spring,'' Morgan said
with a deceptive softness. "Do you think they're going
to look twice at a stiff, sick animal?''

"So I'll walk him now and give him an extra-
thorough rubdown. Why are you getting all bent out
of shape? C'mon, Morgan, look at him. He's healthier than I am.''

It was Eddie's indifference more than his ignorance
that had Morgan shoving him toward the door as if he
were contagious. "I warned you last month after you
let Dancer's Prize too close to Kate Beaumont's mount
that you had to straighten up, and fast. Apparently
you didn't believe me when I said I don't normally give
second chances. I sure as hell don't give thirds.''

"What do you mean?"

"Go pack your things. I want you out of here in an hour. Spud will write you a check to cover your wages and severance pay."

"You can't fire me. You need me!"

"What I 'need' is a good rider. But a good rider has respect for the animal who's doing all the work. You don't know the meaning of the word. Now get off my land. The mere sight of you makes me sick."

He spun around and headed for the house. He had to. If he stayed a moment longer, it would take more than Spud to break him away from the kid. It was the same reason he'd hauled Elizabeth out of her car and driven her home. His temper was shot. Maybe even his sanity.

It was all her fault. All of it.

He stormed through the house and into his study. A footstool got in his way, and he kicked it aside. At that moment he even hated the sight of it.

When he'd purchased Wildwood, he'd bought the furnishings, as well. It had taken a bigger bite out of his savings, but he'd had a point to make. Besides, if he hadn't taken the house lock, stock and barrel, the would place still be empty now. What did he know about furnishing a home such as this? Until a few years ago he had been more used to sleeping in cheap motel rooms, on a cot set up in a tack room; even a couple of hay bales would do. Old wounds might have made him ambitious, but they hadn't taught him to see the difference between the Chippendale couch he stepped around and the two Louis XV chairs facing it.

Disgusted with himself and still boiling with anger, he went straight for the bar. But as he reached for one of the lead crystal tumblers, he froze.

One wouldn't be enough, Deveroux. And as your mother proved, it's not a cure for your troubles, but a demon all its own.

He withdrew his hand and took a cautionary step backward. As he exhaled shakily, he rubbed his hands over his still-damp face.

Put it into perspective, he told himself. The kid wasn't worth it. Hadn't he had reservations when he'd hired him? Hadn't he warned himself to expect nothing? His mistake had been to see himself in the young drifter and to remember how things had changed when Teddy Beaumont had given *him* a chance so many years ago. The difference was that Sawyer, despite his potential, had a bad habit of thinking that the river of opportunity was an unending source, no matter how often he drank from it. Worse, he had a dangerous perception that it was a given, an inalienable right.

Dancer's Prize would be all right, Morgan assured himself. He would keep an eye on the stallion himself, work with him throughout the night, if necessary. Undoubtedly it would cost more than he could afford to find another rider, but what kind of price tag could he put on dependability and respect? If he hadn't been preoccupied with thoughts of Elizabeth, he would have— Damn the woman, he *still* would have been mad as hell.

Even now the mere thought of her made his insides feel as if a giant hand were crushing him. Why did everything always have to come back to Elizabeth? Even at sixteen she'd had the ability to get under his skin like a fine splinter—by the time you realize it's not dismissable, it's invariably become infected. He had been four years older than her, a lifetime more experienced, but he hadn't understood how deeply she'd gotten to him until it was too late.

Despite her youth, there had been something so regal about her, so untouchable. She had class, the kind you couldn't buy or learn in a book. The kind that grated on his nerves, because it reminded him of too many bad memories. At first he was abrupt with her, hoping to simply avoid her. Then it became a challenge to see how much needling she could take before she went crying to Big Daddy. Of course, he'd underestimated her; she never told. He tried to hate her for that. Even as he admired her, he resented her for putting a flaw in his theory that the *haves* of the world were the parasites to the *have-nots*. Then came the day, the instant when he realized he wanted her, and he learned there were levels of torture he hadn't imagined.

She'd just turned eighteen, and Teddy threw her a big bash to celebrate. All the noise kept Morgan awake, and he was taking a walk around the duck pond when he heard an argument. Elizabeth and her date had gone for a stroll, too, but apparently her date had decided he wanted more.

Morgan meant to turn around, walk away, but the sound of ripping cloth made him see red. Within seconds he'd sent the boy running to tend a bloody lip and was giving Elizabeth the lecture he thought she deserved.

"Morgan...please," she whispered, tears streaming down her face. Her eyes said far more than the most eloquent of words. They always did.

Swearing, he took her into his arms. He forgot that he was shirtless, and she forgot that her gown was torn. He became aware how soft, how incredibly good her skin felt against his, and how, when she lifted her eyes to his, he found himself unable to breathe or think.

Suddenly he knew. So did she.

The tension between them only grew after that. She couldn't keep her eyes off him, and he couldn't keep his eyes off her. If she'd been around every day, he didn't know if he could have kept himself under control. But Teddy made sure his girls got their education, leaving Morgan to suffer through weekends and holidays. It was the only thing that kept him sane— until the first time he threw caution to the wind and kissed her. From that moment on he lived in a divided hell, where he alternately berated himself for wanting her and drove himself crazy, thinking of someone else touching her.

Hell . . . He hadn't known the meaning of the word until the night he overheard the announcement that she was going to marry Kirkland.

Morgan took another deep breath and paced across the width of the study and back again. She deserved to know a little of what that had felt like. That was one reason he'd returned to Georgia—not to let it all start again. But history seemed intent on repeating itself. He hadn't been able to keep his hands off her, and now— now he realized it was too late.

He ached. If only he could ease the ache.

Finding himself back in front of the bar, he gave in to temptation and poured himself two fingers of bourbon from the crystal decanter. As he raised the glass to his lips, he heard a sharply indrawn breath behind him. Turning, he saw Spud.

"Miguel's taking care of Dancer, so I thought I'd come and write that check," the older man said, limping over to the desk. For what seemed an eternity, the pen scratching across paper was the only sound in the room. Finally he tore the check out of the book and started to leave. At the door he hesitated. "Do you really think that's going to fix anything?"

When he was gone, Morgan looked down at the amber liquid in his glass. The scent of fermented grain alone made his stomach roll.

With a vicious curse, Morgan flung the glass into the stone fireplace.

Three

"I hate to sound like a wet blanket," Elizabeth murmured, as she discreetly eased up beside her sister and brother-in-law, "and I know you've only been back from your honeymoon for less than two weeks, but do either of you remember that you're the host and hostess of this gathering?"

Katherine Beaumont-Channing popped the rest of the pâté-laden cracker she'd been feeding her husband into his mouth and topped it with a quick kiss, before giving her older sister a tolerant smile. "The chef's protesting that the food is disappearing faster than he can replace it, and I understand the waiters are already running the dishwasher because they're low on glasses. Relax, Liz. You know what they say. 'If it ain't broken, don't fix it.'"

"Elizabeth's only trying to help ensure that our open house is a success, darling," Giles reminded her as he stroked the back of his index finger along her jaw.

"How you pulled it off with the place in this condition is still beyond me," Elizabeth said, glancing around the high-ceilinged living room of the house that had once been a famous artist's residence. "People usually throw an open house after renovations are completed, not during." Scaffolding lined one wall. Another wall was already painted a warm sand tone but was otherwise bare. Kate's idea of camouflaging the whole thing had been to accent it. Linen tie-dyed in Santa Fe colors draped the scaffolding, potted cacti adorned the windowsills, a doorway, even the fireplace. To Elizabeth's amazement, it worked. How, she mused, wryly eyeing the centerpiece of a cattle skull swathed in grapevines on the buffet table, was still a mystery, but it worked.

"People get tired of the same stuffy parties," Kate said, glancing around the crowded room that was buzzing with lively conversation. She gestured toward the lone guitarist sitting in the corner beside a giant yucca. His soft strumming, meant only to fill any lulls in the conversation, was earning him a small, but appreciative audience. "Isn't Miguel wonderful? He works for Morgan."

"How nice for him," Elizabeth replied, averting her gaze, even though she'd been enjoying the music.

"Not for long, from the looks of things," Giles injected, nodding at one of the listeners. "What do you want to bet West tries to hire the lad out from under your friend to play at his restaurant?"

His wife took a closer look. "Oh, dear... I think you're right. Morgan wouldn't thank me for that. He's already shorthanded, what with recently having to fire one of his riders. You remember the one I'm talking about, darling. Eddie somebody—he rode Dancer's Prize at the benefit show. That's the stallion who thought he'd take on Zulu while I was still in the saddle."

Giles's pale green eyes flashed with emotion. "I remember, and all I can say is good for Deveroux."

Giving him an intimate smile, Kate turned back to consider her guests. "Maybe I should go warn Morgan. It wouldn't be the first time Jerry West tried something like that." But as she scanned the room, a perplexed frown replaced her smile. "Where has he sneaked off to? I was talking to him only a few minutes ago."

"Which is more than you've done to your other guests," Elizabeth murmured pointedly, glad to be able to bring the conversation around full circle.

Seemingly oblivious to the comment, Kate glanced at her older sister. "Have you seen Morgan in the last few minutes?"

The question was innocently put—too much so. Elizabeth took a careful sip of her champagne before replying. "You know perfectly well that I've been avoiding the man as diligently as I've been trying to stay out from beneath all this scaffolding. Why you felt the compulsion to invite him in the first place is beyond me."

"He's a friend, Liz. What's more, I want to help him make his business a success. He developed quite an impressive reputation as a breeder in Kentucky, but no one knows him here. I told him to use this party to mingle, make new contacts."

"Perhaps you'd do well to follow your own advice," Elizabeth said as amiably as she could, despite her strong feelings about Kate helping Morgan. "You're now the wife of one of Atlanta's most prominent developers. Have you spent a few minutes to talk to Hugh Nelson and his wife? It wouldn't hurt, considering Hugh's bank is carrying the loan on Beaumont Center."

"For which he's collecting two percent over the prime rate. Daddy deserved a better deal.... After all, the family keeps a tidy bit of change there."

"Katherine, really. Someone might hear you and think you're serious."

"I am."

Fingering her pearl and diamond earring, Elizabeth sighed. "Why did I think marriage would change you?"

Her sister gave her a cheerful hug. "Come on, Liz, stop worrying so much. A party is supposed to be fun, not work. Loosen up."

Loosen up, indeed, Elizabeth thought moments later as she left the newlyweds and eased her way through the crowd. On her sister's behalf she made a point to chat with the family's banker and his wife, then with the architect of Beaumont Center and his date. But all the while she wondered. How was she supposed to loosen up, when every few minutes she felt Morgan's eyes on her?

She hadn't told Kate, but while they were talking, he had been standing only yards behind them. With her luck, her sister would have drawn him into their conversation, and that was the last thing Elizabeth wanted. She'd managed to avoid crossing paths with Morgan since that episode in the car. If it were at all possible, she wanted to keep things that way. But she didn't know if she could stand being stared at for much longer, either.

When next she dared to look for him, she discovered that as she'd worried, he'd moved to join Katherine and Giles. Now all three of them were watching *her*. But it was the look in Morgan's eyes that made her stop the next waiter who passed, carrying a loaded tray of champagne, and exchange her nearly empty glass for a full one.

She didn't know why Kate was concerned about his future, she thought as she took a sip of the wine. Wearing a black sport jacket, white turtleneck sweater and gray slacks, Morgan might dress with more casual flair than most of the executives attending the open house, but he was still the most dramatic, dominating figure in the room. Several women had already noticed him and had strategically placed themselves in his path. Elizabeth wished he would notice one of them instead of continuing this ridiculous cat-and-mouse game with her. Turning her back to him, she found herself almost bumping into her father.

"What luck, Roger. Here she is now." Teddy Beaumont slipped his arm around her shoulders and drew her toward the immaculately groomed man he'd been talking to. "Roger's been complaining he hasn't had a chance to visit with you all evening, my dear. Put the poor soul out of his misery."

"You're a hopeless exaggerator, Dad," Elizabeth murmured with a discreet look of warning. But she graciously accepted Roger Samuels's kiss on her cheek and rewarded the attorney with a polite smile. "How are you, Roger?"

"Fine, thanks. Elizabeth, you're looking lovelier every time I see you."

Teddy beamed proudly as he eyed her burgundy sweater dress. "Isn't she, though? It's good to see you wearing something festive again, my dear. You know, Roger and I were just discussing how long it's been since he and his father had been over for dinner. Do you realize it's been months?"

Elizabeth pretended dismay, while secretly contemplating whether or not she could get away with giving her father a much-deserved nudge with her foot. The old fox, she fumed. Just because he'd successfully married one daughter off, he thought he was on a roll. "I'll have to look into that. How *is* your father, Roger?"

As the attorney enthusiastically went into a detailed monologue, Elizabeth sneaked a glance toward Morgan. He was still with the Channings, a safer distance away than he'd been most of the evening. She almost began to think she could relax, until he leaned over to hear something Kate was saying. As he did so, he shifted his gaze, effortlessly zeroing in on Elizabeth as if an invisible guideline bound them. He made a lazy, head-to-toe survey of her that left her feeling as if that guideline were a thread from her knit dress that he was unraveling inch by inch. Her throat constricted around a sound of protest.

She took another sip of champagne to force it down, wondering how much more she was going to have to take. The man was intentionally trying to make her uncomfortable! She glanced down at her father's watch, almost groaning when she saw how slowly time was passing. It wasn't too early to make a discreet exit, but her father didn't look anywhere near ready to call it a night.

"So if he does get the judicial appointment—and we've been led to believe formal confirmation is a mere technicality—I suppose we'll be looking for a new partner to take his place in the firm," Roger concluded.

"That's splendid," Teddy said, giving the younger man a hearty slap on the back. "Isn't that wonderful, dear?"

Elizabeth automatically flashed Roger the warmest smile she could muster and nodded enthusiastically. Then from the corner of her eye she saw Morgan moving toward them. "Tell your father we're thrilled for him, and that I'll be in touch soon about having you both over so we can celebrate. But—um—you'll have to excuse me. I just remembered I promised Kate I'd check on something for her."

Coward, she scolded herself as she escaped down the hallway leading to the kitchen. She doubted Morgan would follow with her father blocking his path. If Kate was determined to invite Morgan to all her social events, a confrontation was inevitable; but if she had a say in the matter, it wouldn't be now.

As she entered the spacious kitchen, she nodded to the chef, who paused in the middle of a melodramatic argument with the headwaiter to give her a questioning look. She shook her head and was motioning for him to ignore her presence when she spotted a shawl hanging on a brass hook by the back door. She went straight for it, snatched it up and slipped out the stained-glass door.

The night air had a bite to it, though not enough to promise a frost. The moon rising above the treetops was almost full. Elizabeth walked along the brick walkway until the laughter and music from inside melded with the night sounds. Then she took a deep breath of the brisk air and waited for the darkness to envelop and soothe her ragged nerves.

As much as she loved Kate and was thrilled about her marriage to Giles, she hadn't been in the mood to attend this party tonight, nor was she ready for her father to start foisting eligible bachelors on her, as he used to when she was younger. She didn't expect anyone to understand why—she wasn't sure she understood herself. For months now she'd been hiding her true feelings, trying to pretend that she was all right. But she wasn't. Doubts and memories cluttered her mind. She couldn't stop her train of thought, worse, she didn't know how much longer she could go on pretending that she could cope.

Sometimes she felt as though she wanted to run away, from herself more than from anything else. How was she supposed to explain that to anyone? Who would understand Elizabeth Beaumont Kirkland, socialite and heiress, wishing she were anyone but herself for a week or month—or even for one day? More important, whom would she want to be if not herself? Where would she go?

Anywhere... if it meant peace... self-respect.

Hearing the soft lapping of water over rocks, she continued walking until she came to the gate leading to the creek that in the daylight she'd seen just beyond the walled-in backyard. It was a small creek, but scenic; the sound of the water trickling over smooth stones was soothing and—

"Don't go out there."

She spun around, automatically lifting her hand to her throat to stop the cry that was a mere heartbeat away. Morgan stepped out from the shadow of an Italian cypress and came toward her. Obviously he'd come out by another door. She should have known he wouldn't miss an opportunity to get her alone.

"The ground's uneven, and you wouldn't get two yards before you twisted your ankle in those shoes," he continued, when she failed to reply. His voice was low, gravelly—its tone reluctant, as though a part of him resented speaking to her.

Elizabeth drew the borrowed shawl closer. It was warm, but even a full-length mink—though she wouldn't be caught owning one—would be nothing against Morgan's icy censure. "You needn't worry that you'll be forced into making a chivalrous gesture. I wasn't intending on going past this gate."

"Really? I don't think I've ever seen anyone who looked more like a cornered rabbit suddenly discovering a route of escape." He stopped beside her and, leaning against the stone wall, studied her profile. "One can only wonder why? Don't tell me that your friends are boring you?"

Though Elizabeth stiffened, she kept her tone polite. There was, however, no camouflaging the weariness she felt. "I'm not going to argue with you tonight, Morgan. If you've come out here to make a point, then please do so and go."

He didn't want to feel concern. For the past ten years, the mere thought of her had brought feelings that were less civil, even ones of near violence. That was as it should be. Yet there was no missing the aura of fragility about her tonight. The moonlight only enhanced it. She was no less stunning than usual, but there was also a haunted quality about her. He shoved his hands into his pant pockets. "Why were you ashamed to be seen talking to me inside?"

"What?"

"You heard me."

"You're unbelievable."

"That's not an explanation."

Exhaling her exasperation, Elizabeth half turned. "I was not 'ashamed' to talk to you. I simply didn't want to."

"Why?"

"Because this is what happens—we argue—and I'm tired of it. I'm tired of everything." She began to elaborate, felt emotion invade her voice and ducked her head to fight for control. "I'm tired, Morgan."

The impulse to take her into his arms came like sunrise on an early-spring morning. There was no burst of passion as there would be in the heat of summer, but something far more elusive, more promising. Unsettling. He didn't want *her* affecting him that way. It was bad enough that he'd always been a fool where she was concerned; he wasn't prepared to handle feelings beyond desire.

He curled the hands in his pockets into fists and scowled. "What's wrong with you?"

Elizabeth was tempted to laugh. Because she was certain the laughter would turn into tears within seconds, she fought it. There was so much anger between them. "Oh, Morgan..." With a shake of her head, she turned back to listen to the sound of the flowing creek. "Do you ever get fed up—tired of being who you are?"

"It would be a waste of time."

"But what if you were unhappy with how your life was evolving and no matter what you did, it still ended up as flat, meaningless?"

"Is that what this is all about? You've decided your life lacks excitement?"

Stung, she turned to leave. "I should have known better than to think you were willing to listen for a change."

Morgan caught her by her arm. "Wait a minute. Explain."

"Why—so you can ridicule me even more?"

She tried to wrench her arm free, but his hold was unbreakable. Drawing her an inch closer, he studied her face, letting his gaze linger on the shadows beneath her eyes and the pronounced hollows beneath her cheekbones. When he'd first returned to Georgia, he'd immediately noticed she was slimmer than he remembered. He was certain she'd lost more weight since and frowned, realizing his anger over the past had blinded him to that, maybe even more. He wasn't a tender man—but had he grown completely insensitive?

"Don't run away," he said gruffly. "I'll let you go, but don't run away from me."

Slowly he did release her. Despite the warning, Elizabeth was tempted to bolt, but one look at his sharp, resolute expression, and she knew he would stop her, any way it took.

She stepped back against the stone wall—she needed that much—and fixed her gaze on the moon. It was easier. Looking at Morgan brought back too many feelings.

"I won't apologize," he said after several seconds of silence had stretched between them.

"I didn't ask you for an apology."

"Your eyes accuse."

"Don't look at them."

"Hell—can I will myself blind?" With another oath he turned, like her, to watch the moon. Silence stretched again. Finally he closed his eyes. "You have beautiful eyes. When you look at me with...contempt...it does something to me."

He could have confided his most intimate secrets to her, and she wouldn't have been more shocked. Casting him a fleeting, sidelong look, she saw the truth in his moonlit face. It filled her with an indescribable sadness. "I've never looked at you with contempt."

"Disapproval...hatred...it's all the same."

"I wish that just once we could have a simple conversation without lashing out at each other."

"There's too much between us for that."

"I would be willing to try, if you would."

Morgan glanced at her, gauged, decided. "How long have you been feeling 'tired'?"

Elizabeth felt her heart flutter nervously within her breast, and she couldn't quite lift her eyes beyond his strong, squared chin. He'd undoubtedly shaved before coming to the party, yet he still had the dark shadow of a beard. She could remember how masculine, how sensual it had felt to stroke that beard with her fingertips. "A—awhile now. At first I thought it was simply because of—"

"Your husband's sudden death? You can say his name without worrying that I'm going to fly into a jealous rage at the mention of him."

"Lord, you can be so blunt."

"Some of us prefer honesty to lies."

"I never lied to you."

"You made me believe things that weren't true. Isn't that the same thing?"

"What things?"

"That you wanted me, for starters."

"You know I did."

Morgan laughed bitterly. "But not enough. Not enough to make you give up your fancy house or your privileged life-style."

"You weren't offering me anything but a fling, Morgan. I was convenient *and* a novelty."

"And what was I to you?"

Elizabeth drew a deep breath and gripped the wrought-iron gate. "You frightened me...fascinated me. You were unlike any man I'd ever met, and even though I knew it was insanity to have anything to do with you, I couldn't stay away."

"You learned," he replied bitterly, recalling precisely when. "I waited for you that night in the barn. Do you remember?"

How could she forget? Earlier that day she'd gone to the stables, looking for Kate, and had run into him instead. As usual, their conversation was heated. Before she knew it, they were writhing in a fresh pile of hay. They had never had a problem communicating that way. He could have taken her then and there; she was that caught up in him, that far under his spell. If Kate hadn't returned from her ride...

"I remember," Elizabeth whispered. She only had to close her eyes to relive the way it had felt to lie beneath him. Hot, aching, not caring about anything except the next thrilling instant when he would kiss her, touch her.

"We had to stop, but you promised to come to me later that night. I waited and waited. Eventually I walked toward the house—just in time to hear your father announcing your engagement to Kirkland.''

Elizabeth bowed her head and crushed the shawl between her clenched fingers. ''I never meant for you to find out that way, Morgan. Truly I didn't.''

''What do you think would have been more appropriate? Telling me after we spent the night together?''

''No!''

''I've always wondered. How long had you been using me? How long were you burning both ends of the candle?'' he continued bitterly. ''Damn you, you actually had me believing you when you held me at arm's length with that line about being a virgin.''

''I was!'' she cried. ''Dear God, Morgan, you actually believe I knew Daniel was going to propose *that* evening?''

''You had no idea he wanted you?''

He had her there. Elizabeth closed her eyes and prayed for the right words to make him understand. ''Yes, I knew. And knowing that, I never intended for things to get as complicated between you and me as they did. Morgan, admit it, you knew nothing could come of us!''

''Because you'd already determined that I wasn't good enough for you.''

''No! It was because we had nothing between us but a strong physical attraction!''

''A lot of people start out with less.''

''It's not that simple. I had responsibilities. Think, Morgan. My father had no son, no heir to carry on the family name. There were only Kate and myself, and you know what a little mess she was. My father had all his hopes tied up in us. In me.''

"Are you trying to say you married Kirkland out of a sense of responsibility?"

"Partly, yes," she replied, with a proud lift of her chin. He could damn her for it, but she wouldn't apologize. "Daniel and I knew each other for years. We attended the same college, and our families were also friendly. We saw a great deal of each other. My father never made a secret of his hope that something would come of our friendship."

Morgan's muttered comment on that made Elizabeth wince. "It wasn't the way you think! At any rate I meant what I said. I never suspected he would choose that night to propose. Afterward everything went so quickly. There wasn't time to come tell you about it."

"You could have told him no."

"I didn't want to." At his sharp look, Elizabeth made a sound of appeal. "Morgan, I had to end it between us. You terrified me. I didn't recognize myself when I was around you. I had no control."

"You didn't love him."

"Yes, I did," she insisted quietly. "Maybe it wasn't the wild abandon that I experienced with you, but I loved him in a special way."

"Shut up!" With a speed that left her gasping, he grabbed her and jerked her against him. "You were a tease. A spoiled little girl who got in over her head and took the easy way out of a sticky situation."

Elizabeth bravely met his piercing gaze. "You have a right to be angry. I was entirely to blame for not being stronger, and I know now that I hurt you. No, don't try to deny it. I see I did. Before, I suppose I just couldn't believe anyone could get close to you. All the apologies in the world can't make up for that. But if it's any satisfaction, I am deeply ashamed."

"And you think that cleans the slate?"

Something flickered in his gaze, made her heart begin to pound even faster. "It has to, Morgan. It's over, and it's time to put it behind us."

"The hell it is," he muttered, raking his gaze down her body and back up again. "You think you can?"

"I think it's time I went back inside. Someone's bound to be looking for me by now."

But Morgan refused to let her go. "You can't go on as if there's nothing between us. You can't attend the same parties as me, make idle chitchat and see me across the room and not remember."

"No.... I'll always remember."

"Remember and wonder."

"Morgan—"

"All roads lead back to the obvious. I'm back. We're both available...and the chemistry is still combustible. Who can it hurt this time? You can't deny we both have an itch that needs scratching. The kiss in your car proved that."

"You bastard."

Morgan ignored the slice of pain that was cutting through him and summoned a mocking smile. "Yes, ma'am. No doubt about it. But then I never implied otherwise. And if you were as honest as you're making yourself out to be, you'd admit it doesn't matter to you one way or another, as long as I can make you feel alive again."

"Elizabeth? Are you out here?"

At the sound of her father's voice calling from somewhere near the front of the house, Elizabeth spun around. A quick look told her that they were still safe. There was a privacy lattice covered with ivy that protected them from view, but the look she gave Morgan was entreating. "Please, let me go. I don't want him upset, and I don't want to create a scene here at Kate and Giles's."

Because he, too, felt an obligation to Kate, Morgan released her. "All right, go ahead," he murmured, watching her readjust the shawl around her shoulders. "Run. While you still can."

She began to walk away, but had gone only two steps before the impact of his words reached her. She glanced back at him. "I'm not running," she replied coolly. "I'm walking. Just as I always have. Just as I always will."

"Well, enjoy it. Because it's the last time I'll make it easy for you."

Four

―――

"Dad...I want a job."

Teddy Beaumont sank back into the chair he'd just risen from. The welcoming smile on his face wavered, then—as Elizabeth nodded reassurance that she was serious—wilted. "Well, now...er..."

Elizabeth circled the expansive executive desk and gave him a belated hug and kiss in greeting before seating herself on his blotter. "You're shocked. Believe me, I understand. In fact, the last thing I wanted to do was spring this on you here at your office. But as I was driving into town this morning, I looked around and decided what better time to start a new chapter in my life than at the beginning of a new week. I didn't know how else to break it to you without getting straight to the point."

"Been taking lessons from your sister, have you?" Teddy asked, arching a bushy eyebrow.

Elizabeth nibbled on her lower lip before she broke into a slow, wry smile. "It is something Kate would do, isn't it?" She rather liked that, and the more she realized the similarity, the more she appreciated it; after all, Kate had in a way been one of her catalysts.

If it hadn't been for that open house last Friday, she might never have had that strange talk with Morgan. The conversation had made her uneasy and only compounded her unresolved feelings about him, but she'd also come to a profound realization. Only *she* could do something about the quality of her life, and every missed day was a lost opportunity.

"Sweetheart, you do remember Mondays are busy days for me," Teddy began cautiously.

"Of course, Dad. I should have told you at breakfast, but that call you made to your stockbroker seemed to upset you so."

"Me? Upset? I was only reminding the pup to make sure he got me back into the market, while there was still a selection of basement-priced stocks after Friday's plunge."

"'Reminding'? Dad, threatening a man that if he failed you, he wouldn't be able to get a job as a busboy in your building's cafeteria isn't exactly reminding."

Teddy shifted his considerable bulk in his chair before glancing up at her from beneath his furrowed brow. "Well, it worked. But never mind that. What's this nonsense about you wanting a job?"

Elizabeth folded her hands on top of the clutch purse in her lap. "It's not nonsense. I've given the idea considerable thought and I've come to the conclusion that it's what I need to do."

"You need a larger allowance, is that it? Well, you were always a good manager, so I'll talk to your accountant and see he doubles the deposit into your account every month."

Seeing that this was going to be more difficult than she'd thought, Elizabeth moistened her lips. "I don't need more money, Dad. I need to work."

"Sweetheart, people 'need' to earn a living. Between your trust fund and Daniel's estate I don't see how the term applies to you."

"What about emotional needs? Look at yourself. You're financially comfortable, but if you didn't have this office to come to every day so you can growl and threaten, wheel and deal, you wouldn't last six months before you'd be pulling out your hair, or worse."

"It's different for me."

"How is it different?"

"For one thing I'm your father. It's a man's job to be the breadwinner."

"That's the most archaic thing you've ever said!" But reminding herself that her father reacted better when approached calmly and rationally, Elizabeth took a moment to adjust the skirt of her winter-white suit so that it covered her knee. "It's not my intention to ask you to put someone else out of a job, but surely I could do something around here to help out?"

"Can you type?"

"No."

"Use a calculator?"

"What for? You even insist on letting our accountant balance our checkbooks."

"Hmph. For what he charges, he might as well. Can you take dictation?"

"You know very well that I can't.... But I do have good recall."

With a belly-deep sigh, Teddy took one of Elizabeth's hands within both his. "Princess . . . what I'm trying to point out is, you're a Beaumont. I didn't send you to the finest schools so that you could end up doing clerical work."

"Kate has a regular job."

"Don't remind me," he grumbled and wagged his index finger at her. "But since you brought it up, may I remind *you* that it wasn't long ago when you didn't like that idea any better than I did?"

He would remember, Elizabeth thought, lowering her eyes. She could see he was going to be bullheaded about this, but her determination held. "People have a right to change their minds."

Shaking his head, her father stood and cupped her face with his meaty hands. "You know what I think this is all about? You need a lift. Tell you what—" He took her hand, drew her off his desk and led her toward the door. "Clarence is downstairs with the limousine. Why don't you leave me your car and have him drive you and one of your friends to the club for lunch? Afterward go to one of those fancy salons to have a facial or something. Better yet, go buy yourself a pretty bauble to go with that suit."

"But Dad—"

"Nothing like a diamond to change one's perspective."

"I don't want another diamond."

"You're right. Sapphires are more becoming on you. You have your mother's taste, sweetheart. Did I ever tell you how pleased I am about that?" At the door he gave her an affectionate peck on the cheek, but gently yet firmly propelled her out of his office. "Give me a call later, and let me know how it went."

"Dad—"

"No, don't thank me. Just knowing you'll have a good time is thanks enough."

"*Father.*"

The teak door shut, and for a moment the proximity of the brass lettering made her cross-eyed. "You have a nice day, too, Dad," she muttered.

"The only thing he didn't do was pat me on the head," Elizabeth told Kate less than an hour later. She watched her sister set the last cluster of chrysanthemums in the flower bed outside the front door of the Channings' new home.

Kate grinned, but sympathy was in her voice as she replied. "Face it, Liz, you scared him to death. For a moment I was speechless myself."

"It's so enlightening to discover what your family *really* thinks of you."

"Don't start getting regal on me. You know perfectly well what I meant. There...finished," Kate murmured, brushing her gloved hands together. As she eyed the effect the yellow and russet flowers had in accenting the existing shrubbery, she nodded her head in approval. "*Now* we can go in and have lunch."

"I'm not hungry," Elizabeth said for the second time since her arrival. She was beginning to wonder if coming here had been as big a mistake as going to see her father. Since when did she need her sister's advice, anyway? Kate was five years younger, and as a result of their mother's untimely death, Elizabeth had often felt more like a parent than a sibling. It didn't help that they were as different as silk was from denim.

Kate, clearly ignoring the remark, slipped off the gloves and tossed them on top of the basket containing the empty flowerpots. She picked up the basket and angled her head toward the back of the house. "Let's go in that way, so I can set this out of sight until I'm ready to clean up. Besides, if we go through the front, the painters are likely to get a crick in their necks or, worse yet, fall off the scaffolding from gawking at you."

Elizabeth's droll look was wasted on her sister's back she knew. In camel-colored corduroy slacks and a matching, button-neck sweater, Kate was anything but dismissable herself, and there was a happy glow about her that was accented by the swing of her blond ponytail. Marriage, Elizabeth concluded with a bittersweet sigh, was definitely agreeing with her.

"Not that I'm not impressed with this ingratiating show of domesticity, but you haven't mentioned when you're returning to ABA," Elizabeth said, referring to Kate's position as a director of A Better Atlanta, the nonprofit organization that focused on the needs of the underprivileged. "Or are you going to do your own bit of surprising and tell me you're considering retiring?"

"No, not entirely...but I do want to slow down somewhat. There's so much to oversee here, and though I'll admit Giles keeps on top of things, I want to help ease the work load."

"Not even married a month, and already you're sounding like a veteran," Elizabeth teased.

As she led the way into the house, Kate's answering smile was wry. "You and I both know it's new territory for me and that I'm stumbling my way through it. But yes, I like being a wife and homemaker. That doesn't mean that I want to abandon all my work, though. It's a part of who I am."

Elizabeth paused midway in closing the back kitchen door. "Then you should understand what I'm trying to do. I want to find out who—no, I want to develop a better *liking* for who I am." As she continued into the kitchen and placed her black leather purse on a nearby counter, she tried to put her feelings into words. "I feel as though I've stepped out from the Dark Ages, Kate. When I was younger, I knew what I wanted out of life. A home and a husband and children of my own to take care of. It may not have been in style, considering what the magazines were saying women were supposed to be striving for—"

"Hey!" Having just washed her hands in the kitchen sink, Kate ripped a paper towel from its dispenser and swung around to face her sister. "Have you ever heard me advocate cloning?"

"But you have to admit women like me weren't the norm, were we? In fact, for several years we were made to feel pitiable."

"And now society is bemoaning the breakdown of the family unit, high divorce rates, latchkey kids, teen suicides, pregnancies, drug dependency...." Kate's expression was grim as she tossed the wet paper towel into the trash. "Women with your philosophy are now receiving recognition for being the last bastions of a noble cause."

"'You'll have to excuse me if I feel slightly underage to be a bastion," Elizabeth drawled, crossing her arms as she leaned back against the kitchen's island cabinet. "Well, well...this is a phenomenon. It wasn't that long ago when you were spouting a vastly different philosophy.''

''You want an apology? It's yours. I know I used to be a pain, teasing you about being a society queen, and I know we'll always feel differently about certain so-called social obligations, but I realize now that we shouldn't be so critical of each other, just because we chose different life-styles.''

''Remind me to give that husband of yours a big hug next time I see him,'' Elizabeth said, slowly shaking her head in disbelief.

Kate chuckled softly. ''Just don't give him a swollen head. Seriously, though, I do think I understand what you were trying to create with Daniel. But toward the end didn't you see the hint of trouble on the horizon? Daniel's ambition seemed to know no limits. He'd begun to travel more and more.... The children you'd wanted hadn't materialized. You might have had Daddy convinced that you were sublimely happy, but not me.''

''You never said anything.''

Kate glanced away. ''I know, but that didn't mean I didn't worry. And now, even though you're back living at Meadowbrook—and I wholeheartedly approve, because you and Daddy *are* good company for each other—I've been wondering when you were going to realize you needed more. I'm glad to hear you finally have.''

Elizabeth watched her sister give the little shrug that signified she'd said her piece. Kate turned to the refrigerator and took out a bowl of pasta salad, while Elizabeth went to the glass-doored cupboard and took out two plates. ''The problem is, I don't know what to do about it. Dad isn't going to be much help.''

"One failure and you're ready to concede defeat?" Kate asked, pointing to where the napkins and silverware were kept.

As she set two places on the oval oak dinette table, Elizabeth considered her sister's words. "But Dad was right—I don't have any clerical skills. I don't belong in his office."

"You don't want a clerical job, anyway, so why worry about it?"

"Because I'm not qualified for anything else, either. Kate, think about it," she said as her sister placed the salad on the table next to a fresh loaf of French bread and some butter. "The liberal arts course I took in school was interesting but useless. I can plan and carry off the most formal dinner parties, dress appropriately for any occasion, and convince people who like to wax eloquent about things they obviously know nothing about that I find them fascinating.... None of that's of practical use in the real world."

"Would you like a glass of wine with lunch?"

Elizabeth exhaled in frustration. "No, thank you, mineral water will do. Are you listening to me or not?"

Kate shot her a mild look. "Your disposition could use the wine, but water it is. Sit," she directed, retrieving two bottles from the refrigerator. "You're so intent on giving yourself a browbeating about this, you're going to have me depressed in a moment."

She deftly opened the bottles, took two glasses from an antique hutch and, nudging a chair out with her foot, sat down to pour their drinks. "First of all, those abilities you were talking about are a bit more complicated and commendable than you've given yourself credit for. I've met analysts who have a worse track record for getting people to open up than you do and, unlike you, most people who step into an argument in progress find themselves with a black eye for their troubles. As for your college degree ... you're absolutely right. You did take some of the dumbest courses imaginable.''

"Kate!'' Elizabeth nearly dropped the glass she'd reached for. Then she saw the twinkle in her sister's eyes and managed a wry smile. "Thanks for the *almost* compliment. But you see my point? I'm not going to be able to fill out a résumé, let alone get a job with my background.''

"Well, there are jobs, and then there are jobs.'' Kate took Elizabeth's plate and spooned out a portion of the salad. Even though Elizabeth protested, she also added a slice of bread from the basket and slid the butter closer. "Are you willing to work for little or no money?''

"You're not going to suggest I get involved with one of your pet projects, are you? How many times do I have to tell you that I'm not the rebel you are? I don't hand out fliers. ... I don't do sit-ins.''

"Who asked you to?'' Kate gave herself two scoops of salad and eagerly picked up her fork. "I was going to suggest you play big sister to some kids, that's all— or maybe the job might be more appropriately called surrogate mother.''

"I don't know. I do adore children, but are we talking about helping out in a day-care center or something?''

"Or something. ABA underwrites a foster home for children whose parents are unable to take care of them, either because they're in drug rehabilitation programs, they're ill or in prison, whatever. We have a wonderful staff running the place, but as is always the case, better-paying jobs come along and—well, we're shorthanded, as usual."

"I'm not qualified to counsel those children."

"We have doctors to counsel. These children need what all children need. Love. Attention. Someone to push them on a swing or admire their drawings. These kids are starving for everything and anything that has to do with human contact. They need compassion, Liz. That's one of your best qualities."

Elizabeth ingested Kate's words and felt a new respect for her—and a new sense of pride. "You've been working there yourself, haven't you?"

"I try to get out there when I can." Kate watched Elizabeth thoughtfully spread her napkin across her lap. "There's no set routine, and there's diversity. Sometimes you'll find yourself reading to a half-dozen preschoolers, and an hour later you'll be teaching a twelve-year-old the rudiments of operating a skateboard." Kate waited for Elizabeth's double take before chuckling. "I'm only kidding."

"Even so, younger children are one thing," Elizabeth reminded her. "But I'm not sure I'd know how to communicate with a teenager."

"I was a teenager once."

"I rest my case." Elizabeth took a tentative bite of her salad and chewed thoughtfully. "Also it would be terrible to start something like that, build children's hopes and then not continue."

"True. That's why we're very careful about who we bring in. Many of our children leave after four to six months. They're either reunited with their families or placed into individual foster homes. That can be equally stressful for the volunteer who's spent so much time with them."

"I hadn't thought of that."

"There are risks, you should know that up front. Also, should you decide to stay on as a regular worker, I have to warn you that the pay is awful."

"I wouldn't take any money. Even when I was thinking of a job, salary never came into it."

"Then you *are* interested?"

"I don't know, Kate. On the other hand—"

"I have an idea," Kate interjected quickly. "They're having a party for Halloween. It's an all-day affair, beginning with a crafts class where the children will be making their own costumes for the festivities in the evening. Then there's a picnic—if the weather holds—and finally the trick-or-treat party that evening."

"It sounds like an awfully long day."

"And you have other commitments. I understand."

Elizabeth didn't know what hurt more, the quickness with which Kate accepted her hesitation or the inference that she could find anything more important than this. How could she explain that she was simply afraid? "What if I make a mistake, say the wrong thing?"

"There's always staff around to help out. Besides, it's not as though you'll be the only new person there. We often have several volunteers show up for these events."

Elizabeth couldn't deny it sounded like a good idea. At the least it would get her mind off her personal problems. "All right. Count me in."

"I'll phone over there right after lunch and tell them to expect you," Kate said, breaking into a satisfied smile. "Oh, Elizabeth, I can't wait to hear how it goes."

* * *

By eleven o'clock Wednesday morning Elizabeth had decided that things could only get better. She sat on the floor of one of the home's classrooms with two children who, having decided they were both going to be trees for the party that night, were intent on pasting their leaves directly to portions of their anatomies. A half hour ago she'd played referee outside, while they'd argued over the selection of colorful fall foliage scattering the ground. Whatever she'd expected today to be like, reality was proving to be far more wearing.

"Peter...you can't glue that to your eyebrows, either," she said, grabbing the boy's hand as he attempted to do so, anyway.

"Dummy," his sister announced, carefully smearing her paste-covered brush over the back of her leaf. "I have a gooder idea."

"Better," Elizabeth corrected automatically before giving her a wary look. "But not on your chin again, all right, Nancy?"

The towheaded child slowly shook her head. "Not on my chin and not on my nose," she recited in a singsong voice. She looked up from her task to give her brother a superior look. "Look, Peter! I'm gonna be a *real* tree."

Before Elizabeth could react, the child plopped the sticky leaf onto her hair. With a groan of despair, Elizabeth plucked the paste wand out of her hand and scooped the preschooler onto her lap.

"You are a minx, young lady." Carefully peeling the orange leaf free, she pressed it against a sheet of yellow construction paper. "Look—this is what you want to do. We'll glue the leaves to the pretty paper in rows like so.... Then, when we're all through, we'll start another page of a different color and later we'll tape these pages to your sweaters. Isn't that a great idea?''

Peter eagerly snatched up a sheet of construction paper—and his sister's leaves. Her immediate cry of protest should have had the windows rattling.

''Mrs. Kirk*land,* tell him those are *mine!*''

With a silent promise to herself that if she ever had children, she would space them twenty years apart, Elizabeth rose and lifted the child into her arms. ''Let Peter use those leaves, honey, and after we get this paste out of your hair, we'll go find you new ones.'' After getting Peter's assurance that he could work alone for a few moments, she took Nancy to the kitchen area across the room.

Elaine Davis, one of the senior members of the staff, was working on decorating a sheet cake for the party, and gave Elizabeth a commiserating smile. ''Looks like you inherited a live one.''

''If you have any suggestions on how to get this mess out, I'd appreciate it.'' It wasn't the first time today that Elizabeth was asking the pint-size brunette for advice, and so far she'd been a lifesaver.

''There's a pair of scissors in the drawer to your right,'' Elaine replied with a deadpan look.

Startled, Elizabeth looked from her to Nancy's fine, flaxen hair. ''You don't mean cut it off? I couldn't!''

''Relax. I'm kidding, and don't feel like you're the first to go through this. A few weeks ago she got the brilliant idea that she wanted to have red hair like Carly McDermott.'' She nodded to indicate the little girl across the room. ''Instead of helping paint the mural in the hallway, she started using tomato red on her hair. Luckily she started from the bottom up, so we only had to cut off about four inches. Isn't that right, sweet cakes? Keep it up, and you'll have to ask Santa Claus for a wig for Christmas.''

Nancy stuck a paste-covered finger into her mouth and giggled shyly.

"If only I'd been faster, maybe I could have caught her before she did this," Elizabeth said, wondering if she hadn't made a mistake in volunteering, after all. She glanced around the room and saw the other volunteers successfully helping their charges with their costumes. During their introductions she'd learned that many had children of their own; they were veterans at entertaining, using little more than their own imaginations. "I'm not sure I belong here."

"Don't be so hard on yourself," Elaine said, passing the frosting-coated rubber spatula to Nancy and then taking her from Elizabeth. "Here. Let me handle this project. A little peanut butter and a good brushing and we'll have her all fixed up. You can do me a giant favor and see if you can get the lone stranger to join in on the fun."

"Who?" Elizabeth followed Elaine's nod to look out the window where a young girl, no more than eight years old, sat all alone on the swing set. She was all arms and legs like a daddy longlegs spider, and there was something about the way she leaned her forehead against the swing's bulky chain that pulled at Elizabeth's heartstrings.

"That's Rebecca," Elaine murmured. "Mother and father split about a year ago, and the mother's in an alcohol-recovery program. Rebecca's wounded and scared and protecting herself by denying that she's going home in a few more weeks. Want to give her a try?"

Something about the child called to Elizabeth. Before she could do more than murmur her confirmation, she was headed out the back door.

The sky was clear, but the air held a chill. Elizabeth was glad she'd worn a heavy, cable-knit sweater over her soft, turtleneck blouse. In comparison Rebecca looked underdressed with her red sweatshirt. Beneath her dark brown braids, her ears were pink with cold, but the look she gave Elizabeth was mutinous.

"I'm not going in there to make some stupid costume," she announced, even before Elizabeth could say hello.

Her animosity almost gave Elizabeth second thoughts. Then she noticed the tear streaks down the child's face. "Fine," she replied, sitting down on the next swing. "I only came out for some fresh air, anyway. It's been a long time since I've been on one of these."

"They're for kids. You're a grown-up," Rebecca said scornfully.

"How observant. I was trying to keep it a secret, but I suppose there's just no fooling some people. Elizabeth Kirkland," she said, offering her hand. A moment later, when it was ignored, she cleared her throat and pushed herself into a lazy swing. "This is my first day."

"It shows. The others know to leave me alone."

"Why? Are you contagious?" That earned her a look of disgust. "Well, I only wanted to make sure you didn't have the chicken pox or measles or something. A friend of mine is expecting a baby, and I don't want to carry any germs over there."

"I don't have any *germs*. I just don't like people messing with me," Rebecca said reluctantly. "I like being alone."

"Really, you could have fooled me. It's your sad expression," Elizabeth confided in a hushed voice. "And on a pretty face like yours it's a dead giveaway every time."

"I'm not pretty."

Elizabeth's surprise was genuine. "Of course you're pretty. In a few years you're going to be beautiful. Trust me. I may use too much corn syrup in making popcorn balls and have no imagination for thinking up party games, but I do know good bone structure when I see it."

"What are you, a model or something?"

The hint of curiosity and admiration almost made Elizabeth smile. "Well, I have walked down a runway or two," she replied, assuring herself that charity fashion shows did count to a point, if she stretched it far enough.

"People say I look like my mom."

The wistful comment made Elizabeth's heart contract, and she had to fight the impulse to scoop the child into her arms and hold her close. "Really? She must be lovely."

"I guess so...when she's feeling good. But she hasn't felt too good in a while." Rebecca stopped twisting her swing and began the slow, lazy rhythm that matched Elizabeth's. "She drinks."

"I'm sorry," Elizabeth said gently.

"She's at a hospital or something. They say she's going to come get me, but I think they just say that so I'll behave."

"I may be new, but I do recognize that the one thing they won't do here is lie to you. If they told you your mother is getting treatment for her illness, then she is, and she *will* be back."

Rebecca concentrated intensely on her red sneakers. "You think so?"

"Positive. And then the two of you are going to have a chance at a fresh start."

Tears flooded the child's eyes. "I just want to know she's okay."

"Oh, sweetheart..." Elizabeth got off her swing, stopped Rebecca's and slipped down to her knees to embrace the child. "She's fine. They would have told me if she wasn't, so don't you waste another minute worrying." But she encouraged her to cry, to relieve the stress.

After a few minutes, when Rebecca quieted, Elizabeth smoothed the loose tendrils back from her face and kissed her forehead. "There now... feel better?"

"It's stupid to cry."

"It's never stupid to cry. It's stupid to keep tears inside. They can make you sick. Why don't I give you a push, and we'll have those tears dried up in no time?"

"Let's see who can go the highest!" Rebecca cried.

"Hey, that's not fair," Elizabeth said, smiling as she returned to her own swing. "You had a head start."

Suddenly a pair of big, strong hands gripped her waist.

"Maybe you could use some help," Morgan murmured in her ear.

Five

Hi, Morgan!"

Elizabeth shot Rebecca a look. Never had she seen a smile more rife with adoration. How typical of the female reaction to the male. "What are you doing here?" she demanded under her breath, fixing her gaze on the hands gripping her waist.

"Morgan's brought us ponies and horses to ride," Rebecca announced before he could respond. "He's going to let me go first, aren't you, Morgan?"

"That's the plan, Bright Eyes. In fact I was coming over to tell everyone that we're all set and ready to go. But maybe you want to finish your swing ride first."

As he spoke, his breath tickled Elizabeth's ear, and she was helpless to stop the tremor that raced through her. But determined that it be the only admission of awareness he won from her, she carefully extricated herself from his grasp and rose, putting a safe distance between them. "I doubt a swing ride can compete with a pony ride," she began, but as she turned, the last few words seemed to die on her lips. When, she wondered, would she be able to look at him and not feel as though she were in a free fall?

He'd moved, too, and stood casually, leaning back so that one shoulder rested against the swing's durable steel frame. His thumbs were hooked into the belt loops of a perfectly fitted pair of jeans. Like an accomplice, the sunlight accented his strength and vitality, picked up the blue glint in his windblown hair and gentled his hard features. It *was* a trick of the light, she assured herself, an illusion that there was something softer, more tentative about him.

The V-necked sweater beneath his denim jacket matched the highlights in his hair. He wore no shirt, and the hint of powerful chest with its dusting of dark hair compounded Elizabeth's problem of finding someplace safe to look. She wrapped her arms around her waist, annoyed with him for looking the way he did and annoyed with herself for being affected.

"Small world," he murmured.

"One might even say crowded. Are you going to answer my question?"

He slid his gaze to Rebecca and gave her a reassuring wink. "It's as our mutual friend said. I'm providing the four-legged entertainment for this event."

"Since when do you stable ponies?"

"They belong to another farmer. He couldn't come, but he said if I could trailer them over, he'd appreciate them getting a workout. Seems they belong to his kids, but the youngsters are growing up, getting involved with other things like soccer and computers."

"I don't have to ride a pony," Rebecca stated proudly. "Morgan says that since I've ridden before, I can ride a grown-up horse."

Elizabeth forgot about explaining that ponies were a breed all their own as she pictured the child climbing onto a half ton of horseflesh. The blood drained from her face. "I'm not sure that's a good idea, sweetheart. Maybe you should stick with a pony for another few years."

"But Morgan promised!"

"I did," he told Elizabeth quietly. "And I'll be careful with her. As careful as someone should have been with you." He watched as her eyes widened, knowing he'd surprised her. She'd never spoken of her fear of horses to him or how it had come about, but years ago he'd blackmailed Kate into telling him.

When she was only a year or so older than Rebecca, Teddy enrolled Elizabeth in an equitation class. Wanting to make a good impression on the elder Beaumont, the instructor put Elizabeth on his own horse. He'd assured her that it was exceedingly well mannered. Unfortunately he couldn't speak for all his enrollees. When the instructor turned to adjust another student's stirrup, the boy—jealous of Elizabeth's preferential treatment—poked Elizabeth's horse with a pin. The horse screamed and reared back, then took off as if pursued by a pack of hungry wolves. It broke from the ring and took off down a riding path. Elizabeth managed to hang on for a while, but eventually was knocked off by a low-hanging tree branch.

She wasn't seriously hurt, and though she refused to take another lesson, she grew to be a devoted supporter of Kate's accomplishments in equitation. She even enjoyed an occasional visit to the stables to look at the colts and fillies. But she never attempted to ride again.

"How long have you known?" she asked in a barely audible whisper.

"Almost from the beginning." He took in her white turtleneck, violet sweater and matching slacks and thought of how much he liked seeing her dressed casually like this. He especially approved of the wind-kissed color in her cheeks. Yet he reacted most strongly to the touching scene he'd witnessed moments ago. When he saw Elizabeth comforting the tearful child, something inside him had shifted, warmed. "I could have helped you overcome it. I should have. But—" he glanced away "—I couldn't afford the emotional investment."

Elizabeth stared, dumbstruck. He could have just handed her a bouquet of long-stemmed roses, and she wouldn't have been more surprised. But seeing Rebecca edge closer to watch, she realized this was hardly the conversation to be having in the company of a stranger, let alone a little girl.

Self-consciously tucking her hair behind her ear, she glanced down at the child. "Mmm—sweetheart, why don't you run inside and tell Mrs. Davis that Mr. Deveroux is ready, all right?"

"Okay." Rebecca turned back to Morgan. "You'll wait for me?"

"Count on it."

When the child was out of earshot, Elizabeth returned her attention to Morgan. Alone with him, she felt . . . not exactly awkward, but unsettled, now more than ever. Normally never at a loss for polite conversation, she found herself groping for something to say and discovered that curiosity was her most honest reaction.

"What's going on, Morgan?"

"What do you mean?"

"I don't know how to act around you when you're kind to me."

Because he was feeling somewhat awkward himself, there was a slight hesitation before he commented on that. "It's what you asked for the night we spoke, isn't it?"

One should always be careful of what one asked for, Elizabeth mused, deciding to retreat, at least emotionally, from the web of intimacy he'd woven. "I had no idea you were into volunteer work."

Fool, Morgan chided himself. What had made him think that she could want anything from him but miles of space? "What's the difficult part to believe?" he drawled sardonically. "That I'm generous with my time, or that I could possibly care about people who are hurting?"

"I didn't mean that."

"What did you mean?"

"Morgan, I think it's very generous of you to want to do something for someone else. I'm just—curious. Why this particular organization?"

He thought of all the reasons he could give her and then settled on the simplest. "Kate was looking for someone who could supply some horses."

"Kate..." Suspicious of a setup, Elizabeth frowned.

"Worried she's up to something?"

"Perhaps you should be, too."

Morgan let his gaze roam over her patrician features and thought about the man her father had chosen for her. "People only act on things if they're what they wanted in the first place."

Elizabeth averted her own gaze, glancing back toward the building and wishing Elaine would bring the children. It was always stressful to be alone with Morgan, and even more so when most everything he said was either innuendo or accusation. "Is this your first visit to the home?"

"Yes. Yours?"

With a self-deprecating laugh, she indicated the glue and dirty finger smudges on her slacks. "Don't you think I would have worn painter's coveralls if I'd known it was going to be like this? I'm not even sure they'll want me back. There's a little girl inside who might be sporting a butch haircut by now because I wasn't intuitive enough to know what she was up to."

"You seemed to know how to handle Rebecca," Morgan said, his voice so low it seemed to rumble.

Elizabeth felt a crazy surge of pleasure and hugged her shoulders as she gave a self-conscious shrug. "I winged it."

"She opened up to you more than she opened up to me when I first arrived and was looking for a supervisor to tell me where to set up."

"You should have heard her when I first came out. For you she was all sparkling eyes and toothy grin. I wonder what it is about the female species that makes them so much more aware of themselves than males, even at that age."

"Were you like that?"

Lifting her face to the sun, Elizabeth laughed softly. "I was worse."

"You don't sound overly repentant," he drawled, drinking in the sound of her laughter and the touch of remembered mischief lighting her eyes. A part of him wished he'd known her as a child. Would she have bewitched him even then?

"I soon changed," Elizabeth murmured sadly. "My mother passed away, and I grew up rather quickly. Almost overnight life became serious." Giving herself a mental shake, she smiled at him. "At the risk of breaking the spell, do you realize we're actually speaking civilly to each other?"

He more than realized it. For the last five minutes he'd felt as if he were trying to tiptoe on eggshells. Sardonically he replied, "Will wonders never cease?"

His sarcasm stung, and Elizabeth hugged herself more tightly. "I liked it," she whispered.

If they had been anywhere else at that moment, he would have covered the few yards between them, swept her into his arms and kissed her until his senses were flooded with her and the ache was gone. No one made him aware of his aloneness as profoundly as she did. He still resented the power that gave her, but he felt wonder, too.

"Elizabeth . . ." His sigh held frustration as well as weariness. "I'm no good at small talk."

She didn't know how to respond to that. As far as she was concerned, there was an undercurrent of something important rippling between them. It hardly qualified as small talk. Before she could tell him that, however, the door behind her burst open and a throng of cheering, laughing children raced toward them.

Though there were a number of teachers and volunteers, it took all of them to lead the children to the two dilapidated corrals where Morgan, Spud and a helper had unloaded the animals from the trailers. The children were then divided into two groups; those who were older or had some experience in riding were lined up by the horses; those who were younger and had never been near a horse were lined up by the ponies.

Since Elizabeth wasn't about to get near the animals if she could help it, she was the first to volunteer to stay with the waiting children and let the other adults supervise the riding. That also gave her an opportunity to covertly watch Morgan.

Back when he'd worked for her father, she'd secretly been envious of Kate and her easy rapport with him. Now as she watched him instruct the children, she was reminded of those days. How odd, she thought, as he brushed a young girl's shaggy bangs out of her eyes. She'd never imagined him having the patience or interest to deal with children. Yet as the seemingly endless line of youngsters was escorted around the ring, he never raised his voice above a gruff, but reassuring rumble, and there was always a pat on the back for the boys and a heart-tripping wink for the girls. Why couldn't he have been as understanding and patient with her? Maybe if he'd shown her half the kindness he was exhibiting to these children, things could have been different.

"Mrs. Kirkland! I want Mrs. Kirkland."

Elizabeth turned to see it was Nancy's turn to be helped onto a pony. But the child was squirming away from the woman trying to lead her to the disinterested animal. Breaking free, she stumbled over to Elizabeth and tugged her toward the ring.

"No, sweetheart," Elizabeth said, trying not to let her anxiety show. The pony looked docile enough, but she still tried to ease her hand out of the child's firm, sticky grip. "Mrs. Allen will help you. My job is to stay here with the children who are still waiting for a turn."

"I want *you* to help me," Nancy whined, her cherub-round face growing stormy in her determination.

Whether the beast was docile or not, the last thing Elizabeth wanted to do was get near it. Old fears were still too firmly embedded in her memory, and the look she shot the other woman was entreating.

"It's no problem," Lois Allen replied, clearly mistaking the silent message. "I'll take your post this round, and you can guide her around the ring."

"Oh, but—"

"Please, Mrs. Kirkland?" Nancy cried.

Elizabeth glanced around, uncomfortably aware they were beginning to attract more than their share of attention. Taking a deep breath and telling herself she should take Nancy's insistence as a compliment, she gave her what she hoped was a credible smile and let herself be led toward the pony.

"Now you hold him while I get on," Nancy said, happily climbing onto the wooden crate someone had creatively supplied to help the shorter children.

Lois passed the reins to Elizabeth, who first had to wipe her palms against her slacks. As if it could feel her inner terror, the pony snorted and tried to jerk free, eyeing her through a tangled, blond mane. Elizabeth could have sworn she'd seen the same mischievous gleam in Nancy's eyes only a short time ago.

"Nice horsey. Let's try to get through this with as much dignity as possible, hmm?" Elizabeth murmured, putting as much distance between the animal and herself as the reins allowed. She glanced up at

Nancy, who was settled in the saddle and had a firm grip on the pommel. "Ready, dear?"

Nancy gave her an energetic nod of affirmation, but then to Elizabeth's horror lifted both legs and kicked the pony with all her might. "Giddap!" she shouted.

The pony made a startled lunge, jerking Elizabeth off balance and half dragging her with him for several yards. Only an underlying concern for Nancy's safety made Elizabeth keep her fingers in a death grip on the reins.

She didn't see Morgan leap over the fence that separated one set of riders from another, but suddenly strong arms were lifting and steadying her. Too relieved to care about how it looked, she leaned back to absorb the strength of his rock-solid body.

"Easy does it." His voice was a low caress for her ears only. "You don't want him to sense your fear. Reach over and give him a soothing pat, to let him know you're still in control and that he needs to follow your directions."

Elizabeth had to swallow a mouthful of dust before she could speak. "I think I'd rather find the nearest bar and order a double martini."

Morgan's chest shook with his silent laughter. But instead of replying, he placed his hand over hers and guided her into doing as he'd instructed. "You're doing great," he said in the same rich, soothing tone.

A faint tremor—Elizabeth was determined to call it aftershock—raced through her. "Morgan, take over for me. I can't do this."

"Yes, you can, because I'll be right beside you, and you know that I'm not going to let anything happen to you, don't you?"

She told herself that it was insane, but she would have sworn the words were a promise that had little to do with the incident at hand. Almost forgetting that they had an audience, she looked at him over her shoulder.

He gave her only the hint of a smile before focusing his attention on Nancy. "Okay, sunshine, time for some ground rules. This is a pony, not a beanbag. He reacts to being kicked in the ribs the same way you would."

"I'm sorry," Nancy replied, ducking her head and casting them a repentant look from beneath her tawny lashes. "Do I have to get down?"

"Does she have to get down, Mrs. Kirkland?" Morgan asked Elizabeth.

It would have been wonderful to say yes, and Elizabeth felt the temptation as strongly as she'd ever felt anything in her life. Morgan had only to gently squeeze her shoulders, however, and she felt the rejuvenating strength of him seep into her.

"N-no, sweetheart," she told the anxious child. "You haven't had your turn yet, have you?" Readjusting her hold on the reins, she took a tentative step, then waited. Morgan came up beside her. She didn't look at him, because she had the most ridiculous feeling that if she did, she would start crying. But there was no stopping the slow, shaky expulsion of a long-held breath. Then she continued to lead the pony around the ring.

He knew he should have left after the rides were over. There was work to do back at Wildwood, and there was no reason for him to stay. None, except the gnawing need to steal a few more minutes with her.

When Elaine Davis invited him to join their picnic, he had every intention of declining; after all, it was one thing to fantasize and entirely another to set oneself up to play the king of fools.

Then he looked at Elizabeth, who'd stood within earshot, saw her hesitant, almost shy nod. After suffering through Spud's muttered opinion about mixing women and business, he sent him and their helper to return the ponies, telling them that he would follow shortly with the horses.

Later, if someone had asked him how he'd ended up on Elizabeth's blanket, sharing the picnic lunch she'd brought, he wouldn't have had an explanation. Undoubtedly he'd simply followed her, and everyone was either too amused or polite to say anything. He drew out the toothpick topped by an ornamental black cat from a quarter of his turkey sandwich and twirled the decoration between his fingers, allowing himself a dry smile.

Elizabeth saw the fleeting expression and nibbled at her lower lip. "I have ham and cheese, as well, if you'd prefer one of those."

"What? No, I was just thinking.... I guess I've never been to a Halloween picnic before."

She considered the four children who were also sharing the blanket. They were happily preoccupied with their own lunches and conversations. A slightly more rambunctious group than she'd anticipated, but she was getting used to that. What about Morgan? Though he had exhibited a surprising amount of patience during the rides, maybe the novelty was beginning to wear.

"They told me to be creative but to keep the food simple," she said with forced cheerfulness as she unwrapped a sandwich of her own.

"Right. I doubt watercress sandwiches would have gone over very well."

Elizabeth paused, wondering if that was a jab. "There's not much you can do with potato chips, but I think they'll like the jack-o'-lantern cupcakes. Of course, *you* needn't feel obligated to eat any if you don't want to. That tangerine-orange frosting doesn't look as appetizing as it did in the store."

"Everything looks fine."

"It's rather ordinary, really."

"Elizabeth."

Her heart did a crazy, skittering dance. He'd always avoided using her name if he could, but this was the second time he'd spoken it today. Both times she'd experienced the same heart-thumping, nerve-straining reaction, because both times it had been dragged out of him like a plea or a prayer.

She put down her sandwich, aware that it would only taste like rubber between cardboard if she tried to eat it, and focused on Nancy, who was trying to con Peter into exchanging her chips for his cupcake. But every part of her was excruciatingly tuned to Morgan. "I don't want you to be sorry you stayed."

"I will be if I'm making you nervous."

He would have to move out of Georgia to cure that. "You could help by talking to me. Not small talk," she said quickly, remembering what he'd said before. "But you could tell me what you're really thinking."

A good portion of it was X-rated, and not only wouldn't she thank him for that, she would have a hell of a time trying to close her hands over four pairs of ears at once. Thinking about that, he looked at the children and thought about his own past. It was a good thing the ABA people were doing here. Maybe if there had been someplace like this to go when he was a kid, he might not have turned into the hard case he was.

"Are you planning to work here regularly?" he asked after a moment.

"I don't know. I mean I'd like to—if they'll have me."

For years he'd thought of her as almost too confident for her own good. To hear the timbre of uncertainty in her voice now made him want to reach out, reassure. That, too, was a new experience. "They'll have you. You've already got four votes in your favor," he said, nodding to the youngsters devouring their food.

"You seem so comfortable around them yourself, yet I'd never pictured you as a man who liked children."

"There was a time I might have agreed with you." He looked to make sure their younger lunch companions weren't interested in the adult conversation. "But now . . . I know what these kids are feeling," he said with a shrug. Shifting to reach into the small cooler for a soft drink, he popped the flip top and took a long drink. Talking about it proved harder than he'd anticipated, but maybe it was time. "I never had much of a home life," he told her. "My parents never married. My old man was some guy my mother picked up in the New Orleans bar where she'd worked. He was a regular. Well-to-do."

And married? Morgan's bitter expression saved Elizabeth from having to ask. "He wouldn't help her

when he found out about her condition?" she asked
instead.

"Sure he helped her. He gave her money to—" he
shot a glance at the children "—fix things. She only
kept me because she thought he might change his
mind, not because she had strong maternal in-
stincts."

"You had to have been deeply hurt."

He dismissed that with another shrug. "If you're
smart, you develop thick skin."

But not impenetrable skin, she thought, absorbing
this revelation. "It must have been difficult for her to
have to see this man come into the—into where she
worked. Did he know about you?"

"A pregnant woman can hide things only so long.
Eventually he stopped going there. My mother grew
despondent, she began to drink, even on the job. She
got fired and moved on to another place. When she
was fired there, we moved to another city. We never
stayed anywhere for more than a couple years, and
pretty soon I smartened up to her promises that this
time things were going to be better."

Elizabeth felt a lump grow in her throat and got her
own can of soda, also checking to see that the children didn't need anything. "Is that where you went on
weekends when you were at Meadowbrook? To see
her?"

The muscles along Morgan's jaw grew taut. "Jackson talks too much."

"He's our foreman. It was and is his job to keep my
father informed of what was happening. Besides, he
defended you right until you left."

Morgan rubbed his thumb along the cold, moist can
and considered that. "I didn't ask for his pity or any-

one else's.'' Yet as he reached over to save Rebecca
from spilling her own soda, he knew he wanted Elizabeth to know. Then maybe he could lay it to rest,
once and for all. The other children were deep in a
conversation about who was going to win the prizes at
the party tonight, but when he turned back to Elizabeth he still kept his voice low.

"She was living in Atlanta in a small apartment near
the café where she said she'd found a job. But the job
didn't last six months, and neither did the next one or
the one after that. Most of what I earned went to keep
her rent paid, so that she'd at least have a roof over her
head. Do you think she cared? All she ever did was tell
me that I'd never amount to half what my father was,
that she could be with him, living a decent life like a
real lady, if it wasn't for me.''

"Oh, Lord...'' Oblivious of the laughter and conversation going on around them, Elizabeth laid a
comforting hand on his arm. "How awful. I had no
idea.''

"Would it have changed anything if you had?''

"I would have tried to be more tolerant, less flippant.''

"I wouldn't have given you a chance. You represented everything she wanted in life. Do you know
what that did to me?''

"Mrs. Kirkland, can we go play now?'' Rebecca
asked, already rising to her knees. "We're finished
eating, and you guys are only talking boring, grown-up talk.''

Elizabeth shot a disbelieving look at Morgan. His
answering smile was grim.

"Out of the mouths of babes," he murmured. Then he told Rebecca, "Go on and play—only don't overdo it and give yourselves a stomachache, okay?"

They took off in a flurry of whoops and shrieks. Elizabeth was so embarrassed that she was grateful to be able to busy herself with cleaning up after them. What if one of them repeated what they'd heard to someone else? Surely Morgan didn't think she thought their talk had been boring, too?

Morgan watched her rewrap her untouched sandwich and pack it away. He did the same with his and handed it to her. "I didn't mean to make you lose your appetite."

Tucking the sandwich into the picnic basket, she sat back on her heels. "Oh, Morgan." Didn't he know his story broke her heart? If only she'd known... "Your mother died, didn't she?"

"Yeah."

"I'm glad you told me about it. Also, for what it's worth, I'm truly sorry for whatever unhappiness I added to your life."

He closed his eyes, not trusting himself to respond. Did she have any idea how much her compassion meant to him? How could he tell her that after *her* there had been no life, merely existence? How could he risk allowing himself to be that vulnerable again?

He pushed himself to his feet. "I have to get back. Thanks for—" He paused, found himself drowning in the shimmering pools of her overbright, blue-gray eyes. "I have to go," he said thickly and walked away before she had him begging.

Six

―――――

I thought you had some fancy whatchamacallit to go to?'' Spud grumbled, as he stood in the doorway of the study, where he'd found Morgan slouched low in his chair and staring broodingly into space.

''I changed my mind.''

The older man scrunched up his face and scratched at his permanent five o'clock shadow. ''You've been doing a lot of that ever since you came back from the Halloween thing you did as a favor for Kate. I don't suppose it has anything to do with her sister?''

''I don't want to talk about it.''

''You don't want to talk about it. You don't want to do much of anything, including getting angry at that Trask fellow at the Dangerfield stables for stealing a sale from you. Why, in the old days—''

Morgan swiveled his chair enough to give his friend and business partner a look of warning. "Isn't there something you should be doing?"

"Probably, but you'll have to pardon me if I forget what it is," Spud said with exaggerated politeness. He swept off his hat and, crushing it against his chest, leaned toward Morgan. "See, I'm so busy wondering if you're ever coming back from la la land, I have a hard time trying to remember what needs doing and what's been done."

It was nothing less than he deserved, and Morgan pinched the bridge of his nose, wishing he could explain. But he'd never been one to talk about his problems. That is, he hadn't been—until last week, when he'd opened up to Elizabeth.

With a sigh he turned back to Spud. "I'm sorry for the lousy attitude. You're right about me being useless around here lately."

"All the more reason to get out and get your mind off things."

Morgan allowed a wry smile. "Nice try, pal, but it's not going to work."

"I thought you said that everyone who is anyone was going to be at this party?"

"They are."

"So the press will be there to take pictures of all the people donating to the restoration of that hospital wing, right? Well, you're one of them, and we could use the publicity."

They certainly could. But chances were that Elizabeth would be there, as well. He wasn't ready to face her again. Not after sharing so much about the past. His heart had turned to mush when he'd seen her with Rebecca, and he'd practically bared his soul to her. He felt exposed, vulnerable. More ashamed of his heritage than ever.

"The promise to raffle off one of our less promising mares is hardly front-page news with this crowd. You think they're going to bother with a small fish like me, when they have the likes of the mayor, a professional football quarterback and countless other high-profile celebrities to choose from?" he asked dryly.

Spud wandered over to the bar and poured the one bourbon he allowed himself a day. "If the reporter is a woman, your handsome mug is a shoo-in."

It always amused Morgan to hear his friend's opinion of his looks, when he knew he was about as pretty as a tank. But regardless of that, the thought of having to deal with the press was only slightly less annoying than dressing up to attend a formal social function. He shifted uncomfortably and, intent on changing the subject, asked Spud about the "floating" the vet had done on two of their horses' teeth to rasp off sharp edges. "Did he have any trouble with Lady Gray, since this was her first time?"

"She didn't like the noise much, and you could tell she thought the sensation was kinda strange, but all in all she took it like a real lady." Spud took a sip of his drink before shooting Morgan a sidelong glance. "By the way, I thought you should know that I ran into Sawyer. He's working at the gas station down near the interstate highway."

"So?"

"He asked for his job back." At Morgan's dark look, Spud gestured reassuringly. "I know—I know. I told him you wouldn't change your mind. But I thought you should know that he's storing up some ill feelings about this."

"He can swell up and explode, for all I care," Morgan growled, slumping deeper into his chair.

Spud judiciously let the matter drop and concentrated on swirling the amber liquid in his glass. "You wouldn't have to stay the whole night, if you didn't want to," he said after several moments, continuing with his original train of thought as though there'd been no interruption. "You could casually wander over to whoever the press seemed interested in and—"

"You sound worse than a fairy-tale stepmother, trying to peddle her stepdaughter to the highest bidder."

"There ain't no shame in using a little free publicity when it's there for the taking. If business picks up, we can hire more help. This cooler weather's been aggravating my leg. Another hand would make the workload easier. Beats me how I'm supposed to be foreman and stable hand all at once."

"Oh, hell," Morgan muttered, pushing himself out of his chair. "I suppose it's the only way I'm going to get any peace and quiet."

Spud hid his smile by lifting his glass to his lips. "Wear the black suit. It makes you look distinguished."

"It makes me look like I'm going to a funeral."

"A distinguished funeral."

Morgan stomped upstairs, swearing under his breath.

"Elizabeth, my dear...how's my favorite constituent?"

"Good evening, Mr. Mayor," Elizabeth said, joining the intimate group that stood on the mezzanine leading to the downtown Atlanta hotel's ballroom. She accepted his fatherly buss and touched cheeks with his wife. "Dorothy, so good to see you."

"Hello, my dear. Don't you look divine," the older woman said, clearly admiring Elizabeth's sapphire-blue velvet dress. "I can't remember the last time I was able to wear velvet and not look like I'm packing a five-pound bag of flour on each hip. It's almost enough to make me give up my croissants," she added with a sigh.

"Where's Teddy?" the mayor asked, giving one of his wife's plump hips an affectionate pat. "Dorothy wants to ask him to be her partner in a celebrity golf tournament next spring."

"Oh, Richard." Dorothy shook her head and leaned toward Elizabeth to whisper conspiratorially. "He's determined to give me grief, just because I said that between the two of them, your father was the better putter."

"Well, it's only a charity game," the mayor replied with a twinkle in his eyes. "So, what difference does it make if you win or not?"

"I'll ask you that during the next election," Dorothy replied sweetly.

Elizabeth laughed, enjoying the gentle banter. "I'm sorry to have to prolong this decision-making, but Dad was called out of town on business. However," she added slyly, "I know he'll jump at the chance to play with you, Dorothy, especially when he hears of your regard for his putting."

"Just for that I may not tell him that I'm impressed with the way Beaumont Center's coming along," the mayor said. "We had some Japanese investors touring the city this week, and they were raving over the model Giles had made up for the chamber of commerce's display.''

''Really? He'll be pleased to hear that. By the way, congratulations on mastering the language so quickly. I saw you on the news the other night, when you were presenting them with a key to the city.''

''Wasn't he marvelous?'' Dorothy quipped. ''You couldn't tell that only two days earlier when he was practicing, his goodbye included wishes for an enjoyable swim on their flight home.''

Elizabeth tried not to laugh, but it bubbled up like warm champagne. She touched her fingers to her lips and glanced away to compose herself, only to look directly into Morgan's eyes.

A myriad of emotions sprang up inside her: surprise, attraction, wariness. He had been constantly in her thoughts over the past week as she replayed that afternoon again and again in her mind. She wasn't sure what conclusions she'd come to, but perhaps that was as it should be. Morgan wasn't an easy man to understand, and therefore coming to terms with her feelings about him should take time, too.

He stood toward the right side of the ballroom, and he looked as military-stiff and grim as if he'd been going to his own court-martial. Even as she admired the powerfully attractive figure he cut, she could feel the tension in him radiate across the room. At least in that respect nothing had changed. She felt a surge of compassion and wry amusement, as she often did toward Kate, who was also known to balk at making an obligatory appearance at one of these soirees.

Realizing she was staring, she gave him a cautious smile in greeting. He nodded briefly in answer, before turning away to pick up what seemed to be a glass of mineral water with a twist from the bar.

"What a delightfully dangerous-looking man," Dorothy murmured discreetly, as the mayor shook hands with someone else who'd joined their circle. "Do you suppose he's someone with the hospital?"

Because she was disturbed by his response, Elizabeth was slow to realize that Dorothy had spoken. "No. He's Morgan Deveroux of Wildwood Stables...our new neighbor."

"Ah. That explains the minor earth tremor I felt."

Elizabeth felt embarrassment heat her cheeks. What with working on a number of social committees together over the years, plus attending the same monthly bridge group, they'd developed a warm friendship, despite the difference in their ages. But Elizabeth still wasn't prepared for her friend's comment. "Really, Dorothy. There's nothing—"

"If there's not, there's going to be," the older woman replied sagely. Dragging her eyes from Morgan, she gave Elizabeth a woman-to-woman smile. "And why not? You're free, young and depressingly gorgeous. Don't waste it."

"Don't try to tell me this is the advice you give your own daughter?" Elizabeth drawled, wishing a waiter would walk by. Only minutes ago she'd turned down a glass of champagne, but now her throat and her nerves could use it.

"Christine needs a keeper, not encouragement. In fact I've threatened to manacle her to our safety deposit box in the bank. If I didn't doubt her ability to charm a key out of a guard, I'd be tempted to follow through with it, too." She indulged in a wistful sigh. "I really don't understand it. All four of my boys are a joy, but my one daughter seems determined to put me on sedatives."

"If it's any consolation, Dad said something similar about Kate, and look what's happened to her."

"Hope springs eternal, hmm? All right, I'll give the girl the benefit of the doubt, but don't be surprised if I call you and demand another therapy session, Doctor."

"I'd love an excuse to have lunch with you."

"It's a deal."

Soon afterward Elizabeth excused herself and began to make her way down to and around the huge room, saying hello to acquaintances and pausing to chat with friends she hadn't seen in a while. Several questioned her about her sudden low profile, and she explained about her recent involvement with ABA's foster home. Most were supportive, sincerely happy that she'd found something she wanted to focus serious attention on, but a few couldn't understand why she didn't just write the home a check. To those individuals Elizabeth simply smiled, then moved on, which was what she was in the process of doing when she happened upon Morgan.

Though she was several feet away and because of the din of the party couldn't yet hear what was being said, the set of his jaw had her drawing a quick breath and edging closer to eavesdrop. Seconds later the reason for his mood became crystal clear.

Guy Cummings was holding court. He was the well-known and generally disliked columnist for the city's leading newspaper, a fixture at functions such as these, when his other sources were dry and he was sniffing out a story. He was a man of incredible ego, and tonight that ego needed a court jester. The idea however, that he could see Morgan in the role was laughable—no, deadly, she amended—noting again the look on Morgan's face.

Morgan put down his glass and turned to the writer in the same instant that Elizabeth moved beside him. She placed a calming hand on his arm. "Hello, everyone. Isn't this a wonderful turnout? Guy...what a coincidence. The mayor was talking about you only minutes ago."

The tall, narrow-faced man smiled down his nose at her. "He read my column criticizing his overly chummy attitude with our international visitors, did he?"

"No," Elizabeth said, relishing the moment. "It had to do with parking slots at City Hall and your using his while he was out of town. Again." Not allowing him time to respond, she gave the other three people in the small circle a warm smile. "I see you've all met Morgan. Do you know Kate's so impressed with his prize stallion that she's actually agreed to let Zulu breed with Dancer's Prize's daughter."

"There's a coup," one man murmured with considerable envy. "When I approached her, I did everything but offer her first chance at the foal. She turned me down flat."

"Well, her trust in Morgan goes back years. By the way, had you heard that Dancer's Prize took top honors at the state fair last month?"

The first man eyed Morgan with growing admiration. "Do you have a business card with your number on it, Deveroux? I've been looking for a mount as a Christmas present for my youngest daughter. She wants to follow her brother into the competition ring."

Morgan drew one from an inside pocket and handed it to him. "We're still a small operation, so I'm sure you'll understand if I say I'm more accessible in the evenings." After answering a few more questions, he turned to Elizabeth, took her champagne glass out of her hand and placed it on a nearby stand. "If you'll excuse us," he said smoothly to the group in general. "I'm going to ask this lady to dance before someone else does."

Only the grip with which he held her hand told Elizabeth of his inner, more combustible emotions. Deciding it might be better to face them without an audience, she let him lead the way.

The band was playing a slow, bluesy number. Not exactly music to feud to, she mused, as they wove around the other dancers to claim the farthest corner of the dance floor. She was acutely aware of her accelerating pulse, and when he stopped and drew her into his arms, she was sure he could feel it, too. Only the realization that his was equally unsteady offered any reassurance.

"What did you think you were doing back there?" he inquired, grinding out the words between clenched teeth.

"Helping you."

"Who asked you to?"

"I suppose I should have let you flatten Guy in front of all these people?"

"He deserved it."

"Which overrides everything else? Really, Morgan."

He tightened his hold on her. "Don't you dare arch your eyebrow and start playing lady of the manor with me, or I'll—"

Thanks to her high heels, she was almost at eye level with him and though it cost her, she met his fierce glare coolly. "You'll what?"

Dear heaven, but she made him ache. Morgan let his hungry gaze sweep over her. Her hair was a halo of spun gold, framing a face with luminescent skin and eyes the shade of a stormy sea a man could drown in without regret. He held her gaze with the same fatalism that made him know he would never be free of her.

"Kiss you," he replied at last.

Her pulse leaped and she lowered her lashes, not wanting him to see how vulnerable he could make her with two little words. It had always been that way with him—fury or desire—no middle ground to catch her breath. "Morgan...I hated hearing how Guy was talking to you. But don't you see? He *wanted* you to attack him. It would have reinforced his rude innuendos."

"And I suppose having you fight my battle for me made me look more of a man?"

"This isn't about being macho, this is about functioning in society. *Any* society. Just because you don't like all the rules of the game you've decided to participate in doesn't mean you get to change them. Contrary to what you might think, I don't always like having to be civil to simpletons like Guy Cummings, but it's wise to remember that even simpletons can be dangerous."

She was right, of course. However, that didn't mean he had to like it, and he definitely didn't feel comfortable with her going to battle for him, either. "Why are you being nice to me?" he asked, remembering that it was only days ago that she'd asked him the same question.

Elizabeth remembered, too. "Doesn't one good turn deserve another?"

"Our track record would suggest it was *any* turn."

One song ended and another began. It, too, was slow, but more provocative than sad. "Maybe it's time to acknowledge that that did more harm than good and try something new," she said, after they'd danced through several bars.

Her scent, fleeting and mysterious, flirted with his senses and tangled his nerves. Morgan shook his head, as much to clear it as to negate her answer. "You were right when you said we'd never been friends. I don't know that we ever could be."

"Not if you're continually predisposed to obstinacy."

"You're as stubborn as I am, damn it."

"At least I don't swear at you."

"I wasn't—hell."

A smile tugged at Elizabeth's lips. She was determined to recapture the brief, but appealing truce they'd shared on Halloween. Then again, a few moments of silence might be prudent. Focusing on the music, she glanced around the dance floor and watched others pass. Some glided, some shuffled.... Some, she noted with a touch of wry amusement, could barely stand being near each other. It made her realize how well she and Morgan danced together. His movements were so smooth, almost fluid, it seemed unusual for a man of his powerful build. Finding her gaze drawn to his broad shoulders, she glanced away.

"Nice suit."

"I'll tell Spud you approve."

"I beg your pardon?"

"Among other things he fancies himself my dresser."

A faint line formed between Elizabeth's eyebrows. "He doesn't like me."

"Don't tell me that's something you're going to lose a lot of sleep over?"

She shot him an offended look. "It concerns me, yes."

Once again he found himself being drawn in by her eyes, until the knot tightening in his stomach forced him to take a deep breath. He dragged his gaze away and exhaled. "Well, don't take it personally. It's your gender he's suspicious of."

Because he said it matter-of-factly, she let the comment pass and moved on to other points of curiosity. "How long have you known him?"

"Almost ten years."

"How did you meet?"

He'd been at a racetrack looking for work, but Morgan didn't want to go into that. "Two men were trying to convince him to doctor a horse he was training, so it would lose a race. I helped him out, and in appreciation he suggested I bet all the money I had on the horse. I suppose you could say that it was the beginning of our partnership."

"Was that how he hurt his leg?"

"No. His third wife knocked him off the balcony of their second-story hotel room." At Elizabeth's gasp, he shrugged fatalistically. "She had a volatile temper. That's when he swore off women."

"My God," she whispered. "I would think so." But unfortunately the scene she envisioned was like a comedy she'd seen on TV not long ago, and laughter tickled its way up her throat. "I'm sorry," she moaned, hiding her face in his shoulder. "I know he could have been killed, but—"

"I know," he replied. "It still has its ironically humorous side. He'd be the first to agree with you, and if you ever heard him tell the story, you'd never stop laughing."

"I suppose it is healthier to be able to laugh at your tragedies. When I look back, I wonder if maybe that's the attitude I should have taken when I fell off that horse."

"You were a kid. The prospect of losing your life before you'd barely begun to live it would have scared the hell out of anyone."

Elizabeth lifted her head and stared at him. Was he actually defending her? She'd always assumed, because of his own fearless attitude with the animals, that he thought her reaction immature.

The song ended and they stopped dancing, but Morgan made no move to release her. "That was nice," she said in a barely audible whisper. "Thank you."

"For not stepping on your toes?"

"For letting us walk away from each other without the anger."

"Are you leaving?"

"In a few minutes. My father's out of town, and Clarence is waiting for me outside with the car. He has to get to the airport early to pick up Dad, so I don't want to keep him up any later than necessary."

Morgan cocked an eyebrow. "Aren't odd hours in his job description?"

"Of course," she replied, beginning to withdraw. "But—he's just getting over a cold."

Once again she was managing to touch him with her compassion. Then the band began to play a poignantly familiar tune. Elizabeth's hesitation told him that she remembered it as well as he did. "Are we going to pretend that it's just another song?"

It had been playing on his portable radio that last day, when she'd come into the stables looking for Kate. Over the years, whenever she'd heard it, her body would grow feverish until, at song's end, she was sure that everyone around her was aware of what she was experiencing. Now, trapped by Morgan's onyx stare, there was no slow buildup but an instantaneous searing.

"It's wisest," she managed to say softly.

"You've spent your entire life doing the *wise* thing. Where the hell's it gotten you?"

His name broke from her lips in a whisper of sheer anguish, and she shut her eyes against the tears that sprang up unbidden. Seconds later she heard his muttered oath, and he was drawing her back, closer into his arms.

"I didn't mean it," he breathed against her hair. "Damn it, Elizabeth, I don't mean to strike out at you, and why I do—"

"I know.... Just give me a minute."

He slid the hand at her back under the lush fall of her hair. Her skin was warm and ever so much softer than the velvet, but her neck muscles were knotted with tension. Feeling a bittersweet ache override his frustration, he began a gentle massage. "If only I could have forgotten this...how good it feels to touch you."

His low, raspy voice was as seductive as the music, and Elizabeth gripped his hand as though it was her last link to sanity. In response, Morgan drew it against his heart.

She touched her cheek to his strong, smooth jaw. "It shouldn't feel so right."

"As if it were only ten minutes and not ten years?"

"Yes. But it *has* been that long. . . . And I did hurt you, Morgan."

"You're saying I'm still out for revenge, is that it?"

"Aren't you?" she asked, shifting slightly to search his face.

"It's not that simple anymore."

She touched her lips to his jaw. "Thank you."

"Sweet heaven," he groaned, closing his eyes. "Do that again." She did, and he felt the healing balm of pleasure soothe the gaping hollowness inside him. She had the most sensitizing lips. He remembered the one time he'd got her to unbutton his shirt and nuzzle the hair she'd always seemed so fascinated with. It alone had made him rigid with need. He adjusted his hold of her hand until it lay flat against his chest. "Remember when you did that here?"

The strong beating of his heart against her hand gave her the impetus to reply. "You were the most beautiful man I'd ever seen, and you made me want so much."

He discreetly shifted her hand, sliding her fingers inside his jacket. "You kissed me here . . . wet me."

"Morgan, you shouldn't be—"

"You told me that's what you wanted me to do to you, and I did."

Elizabeth closed her eyes against the memory, but there was no shutting off her mind or her body. Her breasts began to ache for that deft ministration, and deep within her womb she felt a throbbing that even pressing her thighs together didn't assuage. As if he knew, Morgan brought their hips intimately close.

"No, oh, please." The words came out tangled. She wanted him to stop, she wanted him to continue.

"I want you," he whispered, echoing that need.

"There are photographers," she replied, wrestling with herself. "We should—"

"Leave." He caught her chin and, lifting it, forced her to meet his eyes. "I want you," he told her again. "Aren't you ready to admit you want me just as badly?"

Ten years ago she hadn't had the courage to give him her answer straight to his face, and then she had opted to follow her head instead of her heart. Just once, she thought, just once she needed to do something for herself. But when it came to answering, she could barely mouth the word.

It was enough. Lacing his fingers through hers, Morgan led her out of the ballroom.

Seven

Limousines were lined up outside the hotel like a string of black pearls. Elizabeth spotted Clarence talking to another chauffeur and signaled him. They did a brief pantomime as he hooked his thumb in the direction of the car, then she shook her head and crooked her finger.

A rangy man, he loped over and deferentially touched the shiny brim of his cap. "Yes'm?" he wheezed, pocketing the crumpled handkerchief he'd just touched to his nose.

"Miss Beaumont won't be needing your services tonight," Morgan told him before she could speak. "I'll see her home myself."

"Uh—" Clarence slid a cautious look from Elizabeth to Morgan and back again. "Excuse me, ma'am, but you know what Mr. Beaumont told me about taking care of you and Miss Kate?"

"I know the rules my father's set for you, Clarence, and I appreciate your conscientiousness. But I've made my decision. Don't worry about my father," she added with a reassuring smile. "Just go on home and take something for those sniffles before you have a relapse."

"Well—" He shot Morgan another wary look. "I guess I can do that."

After awkwardly wishing her a good night, he left and Morgan watched, torn between annoyance and amusement. "He's protective of you," he murmured thoughtfully.

"Besides being a demanding employer, my father's generous."

"It's more than the money. He likes you."

"He *likes* Kate. I make him nervous. It's not intentional, but—" Feeling as if she were babbling, Elizabeth self-consciously readjusted the velvet and satin shawl that matched her gown. It wasn't the chill in the night air that sent a sudden shiver racing through her; tonight Clarence wasn't the only one experiencing a case of nerves.

"There's still time to call it off."

He'd kept his voice carefully flat, but as Elizabeth turned to Morgan, she knew she had never seen him more tense. Could he be nervous, too? Did he really expect her to change her mind? At the thought of such vulnerability, a feeling of tenderness swept over her and helped to soothe her jangling nerves.

"No, there isn't," she whispered huskily. Clutching the shawl and her evening bag in her left hand, she took hold of his arm with her right. "Not anymore."

Did she have any idea what that meant to him? Morgan's impulse was to sweep her into his arms and run like crazy for his car. As he covered the hand on his sleeve with his own and led her from beneath the lighted canopy to the parking lot, he felt like a sleep-walker, fully expecting the dream to end at any moment, to awaken and find himself alone.

Dread became a new knot in his abdomen. The light-footed click of her heels on the pavement reassured him, as did the warmth of her hand seeping through his jacket and shirt. Still, it wasn't enough and, after he assisted her into the gray sedan and got in on the driver's side, he knew he needed more.

She was preoccupied with fastening her seat belt and he stayed her hands, drew her toward him in a silence-heavy pas de deux. Only their eyes, searching through the almost mystical light, spoke eloquently. Then he found her lips and sought to ease at least the first edge of his hunger. But a low groan rose in his throat when he discovered her own passion matched his, accelerating his urgency, not relieving it.

She tasted like champagne and wild honey, and within seconds his senses were spinning. It took every ounce of control he possessed to rein himself in, and by the time he raised his head to gaze down at her kiss-swollen lips, he knew if he didn't stop now, they would undoubtedly end up spending the night in the city jail. Reluctantly he put her back on her side of the car.

Elizabeth watched him start the engine and back out of the parking slot. Her pulse was pounding in her ears, and yet she was intensely aware of the silence spreading between them. There were so many things they should be talking about. Where was he taking her, for one thing? And would this extinguish or fan the flames between them? Would it matter to him if he knew that on one level she was terrified?

"Would you like music?"

"No, thank you."

He wanted to tell her he was glad she was with him, reach across and take her hand within his. But the words were locked in his throat, and touching her was a luxury he couldn't afford at the moment. So he pressed his foot onto the accelerator and willed the miles to pass quickly.

They could be two strangers, finding themselves forced to share a confinement and discovering neither spoke the other's language, Elizabeth mused. *Two strangers, about to share the ultimate intimacy.* Yet Morgan wasn't a complete stranger to her. In one way she knew him even better than she knew herself. Some people started out with far less. She drew in a deep breath and looked out the passenger window, wondering if they would survive the night.

Morgan drove up the driveway to Wildwood, sensitive to the fact that this was the first time he'd brought a woman to his home. The irony was, he didn't know if it was Elizabeth's first time here. Would she notice that except for the master bedroom, everything was as it had been with the original owner? What would she think?

"Did you know the previous owner?" he asked her.

"I was better acquainted with his wife. After she died, we didn't see much of him. I understand he sold out so he could move closer to his brother in Florida, and who can blame him? The house really is too big for one man."

Belatedly she realized what she'd said and was relieved when Wildwood came into view a moment later. Like Meadowbrook, it was a two-storied structure, though smaller and painted a buttery yellow instead of white. A full porch surrounded it on both levels, but what had Elizabeth drawing her lower lip between her teeth were the lights illuminating several windows throughout the house. Perhaps she'd been hasty in assuming Morgan lived there alone.

He caught her reaction and compressed his mouth into a grim line. "Do you think I would ask you here if there was someone else?"

He hadn't exactly *asked*. "Of course not," she murmured, beginning to feel like the coward she'd been ten years ago. "But—do you have a house-keeper who lives in?"

"No," he replied, unwilling to add that at this point he was cutting corners wherever he could. "I imagine Spud left those lights on for me after he cooked him-self dinner. He prefers to sleep closer to the horses." He stopped just short of adding that she needn't worry about her reputation being sullied, but as he parked beside the walkway leading to the front door and killed the engine, there was no denying the hurt and disap-pointment he experienced. Yet why shouldn't she doubt him? he reminded himself. What had he ever done to encourage her to have faith in him?

His movements were particularly rough as he re-leased his seat belt. Its subsequent sharp recoil made Elizabeth jump in her seat.

"I'm sorry," she murmured after he shot her a searing glance. "Morgan, please don't look at me that way. Don't you understand that I've never done any-thing like this before? Except for Daniel—"

Now, of all times, he didn't want to think about her husband. Her first lover. Morgan shut his eyes briefly, tired of being haunted by that, tired of letting the bit-terness overwhelm his life. Tonight *he* would become her lover. Maybe not the first, but if there was any justice left in this world...what? What was it he wanted to be to her?

Slowly he let out a pent-up breath. "Come inside," he said quietly.

Upon entering the house, he immediately switched off the bright hallway light, leaving only the soft illumination from the outside chandelier and the desk lamp in his study to guide their way. It was suddenly more important that she be comfortable in his home than impressed with what he had achieved. "Would you like a drink?"

"No, thank you." Her gaze met his and darted away. She had the strangest feeling that if she didn't sit down soon, her legs would turn to tapioca. "What I'd really like—could I go upstairs first?"

She needed a few minutes. So did he. "I use the first room on the left."

How she made it up the stairs, she didn't know. She was embarrassingly aware of her damp palm sticking to the handrail the entire trip—she, who'd met royalty and dignitaries without a trace of nervousness—and it didn't help to feel Morgan's eyes watching her every step of the way.

Once she closed the door to his room, she took a deep breath and, exhaling shakily, looked around. The lamp on the bed table was lit, but with its black shade provided only a subdued light. Ordinarily she would have enjoyed a closer examination of the antique furnishings that decorated the large room, but she barely looked at them, just as she hadn't noticed anything else on her way over here. All she could do was stare at the sturdy brass bed with its indigo comforter and powder-blue sheets. It looked cool and crisp. More than adequately large for two people to become tangled in, a taunting voice in her mind whispered.

With a dismissive shake of her head, she placed her purse and shawl on a nearby chair.

Should she undress and get into bed or wait? Would he think her a prude if she left on her teddy? The questions came like a flood, made her feel more and more insecure, until Elizabeth rushed across the room and switched off the lamp to blot them all out.

She stood in the dark panting, as breathless as if she'd sprinted the mile run. She stayed there until her eyes adjusted to the subtle light coming in through the sheer draperies on the French doors. Air, that was what she needed, fresh air. She crossed the room and fiddled with the locks until she could pull open both doors.

A cool, clean breeze rushed over her. Shivering, she wrapped her arms around her waist, then closed her eyes and drew oxygen deep into her lungs, once...twice. Slowly her heartbeat calmed.

She was standing there when Morgan entered the room. Still gazing at the stars patterning the sky, she listened to the rustle of clothing and identified the sounds; the removal of his jacket, his tie being slipped off, shoes being discarded. The sound of his approach made her breath catch in her throat. But when his strong, capable hands took a gentle hold of her shoulders, she sighed with relief. And when his warm breath sifted through her hair and lightly caressed her cheek, she felt the sting of tears of gratitude at the back of her eyes.

"I panicked," she said, wanting to explain. "I didn't know what to do, so I did nothing."

"It's my fault. You needed time, attention."

"But I'm a grown woman, not a child."

"A sensitive woman." He bent to touch his lips to the side of her neck. "At the least I should have told you how beautiful you looked tonight." With a scientist's attention to detail, he inched his hands down her arms, examining the texture of velvet and how it compared to her silky skin. "When I first saw you, I had no words, no breath."

Elizabeth tilted her head to give him better access and let him draw her back completely against his body. He was so strong and warm. It was thrilling to have the cool breeze at her face and his warmth behind her. To make it perfect, she sought his mouth with her own. "Kiss me," she whispered.

With a groan, Morgan pressed his mouth to hers. He wanted nothing less. He wanted to absorb her into himself, fill himself with her. It hurt, he wanted it so badly. In search of relief, he hugged her tight against his aching body. Her trembly response sent a shiver of excitement through him. As he felt the hairs on his arms lift, he licked a whimper from her lips, then thrust his tongue deeply into her mouth, searching for an earthier response.

His kiss was carnal and aroused primal feelings in her she'd never wanted to acknowledge. Never had she kissed anyone back with such abandon, and *never* would she have guessed it would bring her such sheer pleasure.

The kiss went on and on until Morgan was forced to tear his mouth from hers and take a deep breath. The sound was soon echoed by the rasp of her dress's zipper as he drew it to her hips. He slipped the dark velvet from one shoulder and brushed his lips over her creamy-smooth skin, nipped and tasted. "You're my obsession," he muttered, before once again crushing his mouth to hers for another bone-melting kiss.

As she lifted her arms to hold him close, her dress slid to her waist, then to the floor. A breeze whispered through the sheer draperies. Like icy fingers it moved over Elizabeth's bared skin. "Cold," she murmured, turning in Morgan's arms to snuggle against him. "Let's shut the doors."

"Not if it gets you this close," he replied, smiling briefly. The smile died when he ran his hands down her silk-clad body and his face took on the hardened look of a man fighting for control over his desire. "Put your arms around my neck and I'll warm you."

As she did, he slid his arms around her hips and effortlessly carried her to the bed. He lowered her diagonally across it, then covered her with his own body. His sweeping gaze took in the picture she made with her golden hair fanning out over the dark comforter, diamonds sparkling at her ears, midnight-blue silk and lace shimmering against the pearly luster of her skin. Tonight the lady was a pagan princess, and she was his.

"You're more lovely than I remembered," he said thickly, gliding his hand downward in a slow caress from her shoulder to her nylon-clad thigh. His chest expanded with a quickly drawn breath as he watched her body's reaction—the slight arch in her back, the way the silk lovingly molded itself to her swelling breasts and the budlike nipples that were pouting invitingly. Unable to deny himself for a moment longer, he lowered his head and drew one tip into his mouth.

Elizabeth gasped with pleasure. It had been so long since she'd been touched this intimately. She hadn't realized how desperately she'd missed it and she slid her hands deep into his thick hair to savor the scintillating sensations. Each stroke of his tongue, each gentle nibble of his teeth sent her higher, until she felt the heat curl in her womb and she locked her thighs together to prolong the exquisite feeling.

"Morgan—"

"Touch me," he said, shifting to rest on one elbow. He took her hands and placed them inside his half-unbuttoned shirt. "I want to feel your hands on me, too. Yes, like that. *Yes*." The word became a hiss as nimble fingers combed through the springy hair matting his chest, following the dark trail downward until his shirt blocked any farther exploration. Frustrated, she finished undoing the buttons, while he yanked at his cuff links, sending them flying. After he all but tore the shirt off his back and flung it away, he took her on a dizzying ride, rolling over so that suddenly he was on his back and she lay on top of him. "Now," he breathed, shifting her until he was cupped intimately in the juncture of her thighs. "I'm all yours."

He was magnificent, she thought, too preoccupied with that reality to be embarrassed or shy. His body was strong, so different from hers that she couldn't have resisted gliding her hands over his powerful muscles if she'd wanted to. She also enjoyed seeing the way he couldn't hide his body's reactions from her, especially when her fingertips grazed his own nipples. Feeling him jerk beneath her, seeing the plea in his dark eyes, she lowered her head and did for him what moments ago he'd done for her.

She licked him with kittenlike strokes, wetting him, then suckling. It made the fire burning within him burst out of control. Sliding his hands to her hips, he cupped her and rotated her against him once, twice—heard the roar of the inferno echo in his ears and rolled her back beneath him.

"I thought I could take this slow, but I can't," he rasped, drawing the straps of her teddy off her shoulders. "I've waited too long for this...to be inside you. I'm sorry." He punctuated the apology by placing enticing kisses over every inch of skin he exposed.

Elizabeth wanted to tell him it didn't matter, that this was what she wanted, too, but his passion was contagious, and soon their hands were tangling in their frantic attempts to undress each other. It was Morgan who recovered for long enough to reach into his bed table drawer and retrieve what, in saner moments, they both would have acknowledged was necessary. But it was Elizabeth who, wanting somehow to thank him, overcame a fleeting awkwardness to take it from him and turn the clinical act into a sensual sharing.

Morgan knew he was lost.

"Oh, Lord," he groaned, stilling the hand that offered yet another caress. Knowing he was on the brink of losing control, he pressed her deep into the bedding and died a little more as he carefully sought a place for himself inside her. She was so tight...so wet...so warm. He wanted to savor the moment, and yet he couldn't stay still. Something wild was pulling at him, taking over.

"Please," Elizabeth whispered, gliding her hands up and down his back in a restless appeal.

He groaned when she lightly scored his back with her nails, and captured her lips with his. Kissing her deeply, fiercely, he matched the stroking of his tongue to the rhythm of his rocking hips. Hungry, she tried to arch closer, asking for more. Again and again he withdrew before surging powerfully back into her. Sliding his hand between them, he buried his fingers in silky curls and soft woman and feasted on her throaty moan. Breathing became nothing more than ragged panting, their bodies grew feverishly damp, and their hearts beat a single, frantic beat.

Feeling the end nearing for both of them, Morgan lifted his head to gaze down at her. He needed to know she understood whom she was sharing this with. "Look at me," he whispered hoarsely. "When it happens, I want you to—look at me. See me...know this is us...*us*."

She couldn't open her eyes, because it was already beginning for her. Sensations, the indescribable explosions happening within her, tore a gasp and then a cry from her as she clung to him. But it was his name she chanted again and again, and as before, it was enough. Seconds later he experienced his own powerful release.

Nothing would ever be the same again. It was the second thing Morgan realized when the initial trickles of reality penetrated his scorched mind. The first was that while his mental faculties might not be in the best working order, his body was telling him that he was going to be a hungry man again, and very soon.

The fact wasn't lost on Elizabeth, either. Feeling the subtle, but unmistakable evidence inside her, her eyes popped open and she found him watching her with a look that could only be described as predatory. For a brief eternity they simply stared at one another while dozens of thoughts and questions raced through their minds.

If she says one thing about having made a mistake, I might not be able to keep my hands off her neck.

Is he this... virile with every woman he's with? Have there been many? Was it ever anything like this?

Does she know she's turning me on simply by looking at me like that?

Why doesn't he say something?

Why doesn't she say something?

"Am I too heavy?"

Elizabeth managed a brief shake of her head. "It's fine."

"Fine?"

The arrogant lift of his stark eyebrow had a smile tugging at her lips. "Wonderful. Incredible." The smile became a soft gasp when she felt him move inside her. "You're—"

"Mmm."

"Again?"

"Oh, yes. We put this off for ten years. Do you think I can be satisfied in ten minutes?" He couldn't tell her yet, but he already knew he would never stop wanting this, *her*. In a burst of uncontrollable passion, he'd told her that she was his obsession, and though he didn't doubt it had long been true, he was only beginning to get adjusted to the idea himself.

"No," she admitted, slowly reaching up to smooth his hair back from his forehead. "I want you again, too. It's strange." She gazed deeply into his eyes, as if she could find answers in their depths. "If I'd never known you, I'd have believed I wasn't a very passionate person."

"You told me sex was good with your husband."

"It was...tender and warm. But with you—I'm sorry." She lowered her lashes to hide her embarrassment. "I didn't mean to sound like I'm comparing."

"It's all right." When she still refused to look at him, he grasped her chin and forced her. "I want to know. How is it different?"

Mesmerized by his dark, probing gaze, she answered him. "With you it's like I'm riding a roller coaster with no brakes. I'm not sure it's sane to even get on."

"I've got news for you, lady. You're already *on*," he drawled, slowly lowering his mouth to hers as he languidly began once more to move inside her. "Your only option is to hold on and enjoy the ride."

"Morgan—"

"No. No more talking. Not that kind, anyway. You feel like talking, you tell me what turns you on...what you want...if this feels half as good to you as it does to me." He crushed his mouth to hers for an endless, pleasure-seeking kiss that soon had her winding her fingers through his hair. But it wasn't all that got tangled there, and wincing in pain, Morgan wrenched himself free. "And I'll tell you something else we're not going to do again," he muttered, grasping her left wrist. Before she understood what he was up to, he'd removed her wedding ring and slammed it onto the bed table.

Elizabeth looked from the ring to the man watching her. She knew that look of challenge well. When she was sixteen, she'd seen it the first time she'd threatened to have him fired for his audacity. When she was seventeen, she saw it when he told one of her dates to get off a horse the boy really was too inexperienced to ride. When she was eighteen, it was after she told him she would scratch his eyes out, if he ever tried to kiss her again. The list was endless, but the outcome had always been the same. Anger.

Not this time, she vowed, sliding her ringless hands up his chest and over his shoulders to draw him back to her. "I'm cold again," she said huskily. "What are you going to do about it?"

As Morgan gazed down into her blue-gray eyes, he experienced a moment when he would have literally bet the farm that his heart stopped. When it began to beat again, it slammed against his chest like a wrecking ball. Maybe he was turning into a masochist, but nothing had ever felt so perfect.

Carefully framing her face within his hands, he used his thumbs to slowly explore her cheekbones, her chin, to gently coax her lips open to receive the slowest, tongue-tangling kiss he could orchestrate. "I'm going to build the hottest damn fire you've ever experienced right here in this bed," he whispered rawly, when he finally paused to breathe again. "And you're going to help me."

"Then we're going to curl up and sleep in the glowing, red coals?" she asked, exploring the corded muscles stretching across his shoulders...chest... abdomen.

"Until one of us feels a need to fan the fire again."

"Could be a long night."

"Oh, lady, lady, I hope so."

Elizabeth eased her hand to the spot where their bodies were joined and returned the tender ministrations that moments ago he'd bestowed on her. "Me, too, Morgan," she whispered breathlessly. "I don't care if morning ever comes."

Eight

Had it all been a dream? As Elizabeth stood on the front porch of Meadowbrook and watched Morgan's car pull away, she wondered if, the moment she stepped through the front door, she would wake up in her own bed and realize it had all been fantasy. A whimsical smile touched her lips. It was a little past Cinderella's curfew, she mused, watching the sun creep higher on the horizon.

When Morgan's car disappeared from view, she took a deep breath and let herself inside. She wanted to get upstairs and take a long, hot shower, not only because every muscle and bone in her body had decided to wait until now to rebel against those hours of torrid lovemaking, but also because she had a full day ahead of her and she needed to do something to wake up.

It wouldn't hurt to get out of these clothes, either, she reminded herself drolly as she shut the door and tiptoed toward the stairs. She didn't doubt Leona knew she hadn't come home last night. When seven o'clock had rolled around and she hadn't come down for her usual, calorie-conscious fruit cup, Leona inevitably would have gone upstairs and had a minor heart attack upon discovering the bed hadn't been slept in.

Well, she could handle that. Leona's disapproving looks and long-winded mutterings would be nothing compared to what her father would do if he found out. As it was, she was going to have enough trouble when she told him she wouldn't be attending the horse show with him today.

"Elizabeth Jeanette! Where the devil do you think you're going?"

She froze on the first step and shut her eyes. *Murder*. She hadn't heard that much vibrato in his voice since Kate welcomed her first and last reporter and photographer into the house and took them on a tour, which ended abruptly when the entourage walked in on Teddy in his bathtub. But Kate had had an advantage—she'd only been seven at the time.

Elizabeth gripped her purse and shawl to her thumping heart and, fixing a bright smile on her face, spun around. "Dad—what a lovely surprise! I didn't expect you back quite this early."

"Obviously."

"Did you have a good flight?"

"Never mind the flight," Teddy blustered, shifting sideways to gesture into his study. "I want you in here, miss. Now."

"Oh, dear, could it wait? I really am running late."

"Confound it, girl, I said *now*."

His roar sent the foyer's crystal chandelier tinkling musically and brought Leona bursting through the kitchen door. The housekeeper came to an abrupt halt when she saw Elizabeth, and with a narrow-eyed look, she folded her arms over her chest.

"So, you're back."

"Could we do this one lecture at a time, please?" With a sigh of resignation, Elizabeth reached up to brush her hair back behind her ear. It was then she spotted her naked ring finger. Her heart plummeting faster than Southern spirit after Lee's surrender, she swiftly tucked her hand inside the shawl. "Dad, I think we'll table this until you have your temper under control. You know what Dr. Quisenberry said about keeping your blood pressure down."

"How can a man keep his blood pressure down, when he returns to his home and finds his eldest child, his pride and joy, reducing herself to this?"

Elizabeth lifted her eyebrows a fraction of an inch. "What have I reduced myself to?"

"A common, er—"

"Jezebel," Leona supplied helpfully.

Teddy caught the subtle lift of Elizabeth's chin and, clearing his throat, he gripped the lapels of his slightly wrinkled business suit. "Yes, well, staying out all night, not caring who sees you coming home in your evening clothes. I'm only grateful your mother isn't here to see this."

"Oh, for heaven's sake. Dad, I'm thirty years old."

"You're married!"

"Widowed!" she cried back, impulsively thrusting out her ringless hand.

Both Leona and her father gasped. A moment later Leona threw her hands into the air and disappeared into the kitchen. Teddy's coloring turned the shade of his tie, but he remained rooted where he stood.

It was the expression on his face that had Elizabeth coming off the stairs and crossing the foyer to give him the same kind of hug they used to share whenever she returned from school for a holiday. "Please, don't look at me like that. It breaks my heart to think you're displeased with me."

"You were always my perfect princess," he replied gruffly, as if reminiscing.

"Oh, Dad...don't put me on a pedestal. I was never perfect. Anyway," she added more cheerfully, leaning back and pretending to scowl, "what's going on here? Not two months ago you were all but handing Kate to Giles on a silver platter."

Teddy's jowls doubled as he ducked his head in order to avoid her scrutiny. "I did nothing of the kind. I merely wanted Channing to know he had my blessings, in case he was interested."

"Mmm... Why do I think you'd have had armed guards at the airport, if he'd tried to leave town without her? And while we're at it, I'd bet you a case of your favorite bourbon that if I told you it was Roger Samuels who just drove me home, you would be phoning the caterers, instead of acting like a medieval nanny who'd lost track of her charge for twenty-four hours."

"Were you with Samuels?" he asked hopefully.

With a shake of her head, Elizabeth turned back toward the stairs. "This is really going to have to wait. I'm going upstairs to take a quick shower." It was the coward's way out not to tell her father right then and there that she was going to the horse show with Morgan, but she needed a few more minutes to get her bearings and adjust to the idea herself.

Once up in her room, after she'd tossed her shawl and purse onto the bed, she studied her left hand and the white circle on her ring finger that stood out even against her pale skin. She couldn't believe she'd forgotten it on Morgan's bed table. It said a lot about the man and what they'd shared last night.

Her body throbbed with the memory of him. It left little room for anything else, not regret, not embarrassment, not even room to worry if—when—she would see him again. Of his own volition he'd asked her to attend the show with him, and he would be coming back for her in slightly over an hour.

She still couldn't believe it. Not any of it. What was happening to her? To them?

Too dazed to make sense of anything but the desire to see him again, Elizabeth hastily stripped off her clothes and went into the bathroom. She preferred long, languid baths, but she turned on the shower, settling for a hot one. The one concession she allowed herself was to use her most expensive bubble bath instead of soap. She wanted the feel of liquid satin on her body and the lush floral fragrance enveloping her.

When they'd awakened this morning, Morgan had suggested they shower together. Even now the memory of the way he'd phrased the suggestion made her body tingle with renewed awareness, exactly as it had then. Inevitably the shower was postponed and afterward there hadn't been time. As she stepped into the steamy, glass cubicle and under the stinging spray, Elizabeth closed her eyes and imagined what she'd missed. It was incredible—in less than twenty-four hours the man was turning her into an insatiable wanton.

"Child, you fall asleep in there, you'll drown."

Startled, Elizabeth spun around to see the hazy figure of Leona through the shower door. "I—I'm okay. I'll only be a minute or two longer."

"I brought you up a strong cup of coffee and a hot cinnamon roll."

Just the thought of food made her mouth water. When had she last eaten? "Could you lay out my slate-blue suede outfit and the matching boots? I think I'll wear those to the show."

"I'll do it, but you get a move on, hear? Your daddy's already phoned your sister and Mr. Giles. Since she's not competing this time, they're going with y'all."

Lovely, Elizabeth thought, groaning inwardly, that was all she needed—Kate gloating or, worse yet, asking her every kind of question. Why couldn't Giles have had a business trip out of town and taken his wife with him?

Despite hurrying, Elizabeth was late getting downstairs. Even before she got halfway, she could hear her father's thundering and another deep, implacable voice reply.

"I don't give an owl's hoot what she told you, boy, she's a Beaumont. She'll be attending this event with her family and sitting in the Beaumont box. The arrangements were made months ago."

"Mr. Beaumont, with all respect, I don't think there's anything more to discuss."

"Damned straight."

"She's coming with me."

As Elizabeth hurried across the foyer, she could picture her father's expression. She had to get in there before he had a seizure.

"You know what your problem always was, Deveroux? You're as thickheaded as a mule. I don't want my daughter anywhere near you, and she'll obey my wishes."

"May I ask why you don't approve of me, sir?"

"You don't respect rules. You see something you want, you don't go through proper channels, you don't follow established procedure, you just bulldozer in and grab it."

"Something like your own attitude, sir?"

"Insolence! My daughter is *not* an acquisition!"

"You sure treated her like one when you pushed her into marrying Kirkland."

Elizabeth rushed into the study before her father could answer, but she could tell by the florid color of his face that his response would have been tantamount to a volcanic eruption. "Father—how nice of you to entertain Morgan while I was getting ready."

Teddy alternately stretched, then clenched the fingers at his sides. "Elizabeth, kindly tell *Mr.* Deveroux that you'd have to be hog-tied to the trunk of his car or as loony as your dear mother's youngest sister before you'd desert your own blood to go somewhere with the likes of him."

Rather than meet Morgan's cool look of inquiry, she adjusted the shoulder strap on her small, blue suede purse and needlessly smoothed her blouse collar over her bolero-style jacket. "Father, while it distresses me to see you this distraught over my decision, I *did* tell Morgan that I would accompany him today." Before Teddy could reply, she closed the distance between them and laid a finger against his lips. "I have every right to go out with whomever I choose. Now not another word. We've never been rude to a guest in this house, and we won't start now."

After giving him a tender kiss on his cheek and assuring him she'd see him at the arena, she nodded to Morgan and walked out of the study. They'd got no farther than the front porch when they met Kate and Giles.

"I thought I recognized that car," Kate said, affectionately embracing Morgan. "What a wonderful surprise! Are you joining us in the family box?"

"No, I need to get there early and oversee Dancer's care," Morgan replied, smiling as he noted Kate's speculative gaze darting from him to her sister. "My new rider's inexperienced in competition, and Spud takes too much pleasure in intimidating him."

Giles drew Elizabeth's attention and slowly cocked an aristocratic eyebrow. "And I suppose you're going along to make sure Deveroux doesn't intimidate anyone?"

"I adore British humor," Elizabeth murmured, lightly kissing his cheek before giving it a tap with her finger. "It's so droll. You'd better go in and calm Father," she added to Kate. "He's not taking this well."

Kate's eyes lighted with merriment as she grabbed her husband's hand and drew him toward the front door. "Isn't this a riot? All these years Liz was the one having to calm him down for something I'd done. Now I finally get to return the favor. Don't worry, Lizzy, I'll take care of everything."

"Why isn't that consoling?" Elizabeth drawled, continuing toward Morgan's car.

When she was seated inside, she concentrated on securing her seat belt. Morgan got in on the driver's side, but sensitive to the shift in her mood, he ignored his own belt to consider her patrician profile.

"All right, out with it. What's bothering you?"

"Didn't you say you're in a hurry?"

"The hell with that. I want to know what has you as tight as an overwound spring?"

Knowing they wouldn't budge an inch until she told him, Elizabeth shifted to face him. He looked totally in command today in his gray sport jacket and matching slacks. But it was the navy turtleneck sweater that made her pulse accelerate. It emphasized the blue sheen in his freshly washed and blow-dried hair and made his onyx eyes appear like a starless, midnight sky. She had to consciously work at resisting their pull.

"I don't like being forced to choose loyalties," she said with quiet dignity. "Please don't put me in that position again."

Morgan briefly entertained the impulse to forget about the damned horse show and take her back to his house, so they could pick up where they'd left off a few hours ago. With the speed of a cobra he reached out and, gripping the back of her neck, brought her toward him for a stomach-churning, moan-wrangling kiss. Both, he grimly noted, were *his* reactions, but he still took a great deal of pleasure when she blindly sought and, having found them, gripped his wrists with her hands.

"You were saying?" he murmured when he raised his head and focused on her full, trembling lips.

"Morgan, this isn't fair."

"Not much in real life is. If you want out, unfasten your seat belt and grab that door latch. Fast. Otherwise I'm getting the hell out of here."

The next ten seconds of his life felt like a one-way ticket to a rocket-launched nosedive down a mine shaft. When Elizabeth slowly shook her head, he wanted desperately to reach out...take her in his arms...simply hold her. No, not so simply. Deep down he knew it was time to admit that he wouldn't really have let her go, had she tried to leave. That had him shaking inside. An uncomfortable dampness had his sweater clinging to his back. All because he cared. It was more than lust, this thing he felt for her, and having never experienced that with another human being, he was all but quaking in his boots.

Because he wasn't sure he wanted to know how she would respond to *that*, he released her and keyed the ignition. Neither of them said a word as he pulled away from Meadowbrook. But shortly after he turned onto the main road, he'd recovered enough to reach into his jacket and pass her the diamond ring she'd forgotten. Elizabeth took it and, just as silently, dropped it into her purse.

Morgan drove another mile without taking his eyes off the road. In fact neither of them looked at each other again, not even when he reached over and linked his fingers through hers.

"Now whatever you do, don't use him up in the practice run," Spud grumbled to the slenderly built teenager in the formal, black habit. Oblivious to Morgan and Elizabeth's approach, he helped the boy up on the stallion and continued his lecture. "He doesn't need much of a warm-up, and we don't want everyone else to see what they're up against before the competition starts. You call those boots polished? We'll have to work on that after you come in from practice. For the love of heaven, do you think you can do without that gum for a few minutes?''

"Take it easy, Spud,'' Morgan said, grasping the older man's shoulder reassuringly. "Most everyone around here's already familiar with Dancer's capabilities, and Jimmy's going to be fine, aren't you, son?''

The red-haired boy's expression mirrored his relief at Morgan's arrival and his respect. "I'll do my best to make you proud of me, sir.''

"I don't doubt you will. Jim Delaney, I'd like you to meet Elizabeth Beaumont Kirkland. Her sister owns Zulu, the only horse who could have given you serious competition today.''

The boy gave Elizabeth a shy smile. "Ma'am.''

"Delaney? You're not Tucker Delaney's son, are you?'' At the boy's embarrassed but delighted nod, she extended her hand. "My father thinks your father is the best vet in the state. Good luck, Jim. Of course, if Mr. Deveroux trusts you in that saddle, I don't think you need my good wishes.''

"Just as long as you don't forget that you're more expendable than the horse,'' someone added behind her.

Recognizing the voice, Morgan wheeled around to find Eddie Sawyer leaning against their stable door. A sardonic smile framed the matchstick between his teeth. "What are you doing here?'' Morgan demanded, taking a step toward the other man.

Prompted by the fury she heard in his voice, Elizabeth grasped his sleeve. "Morgan,'' she murmured,

taken aback by the violence she saw in his eyes.
"What's wrong?"

He hesitated a moment, before retracing the step
and covering her hand with his own. Elizabeth was
right; this wasn't the place for trouble. A scene would
hurt his reputation more than Sawyer's, and despite
the residual anger Morgan felt toward him, he simply
wasn't worth the trouble it could cause for Wildwood. However, Morgan couldn't help think that
nothing would please him more than to have the assurance that Eddie Sawyer wasn't within a thousand
miles of Dancer's Prize. There was something about
the guy...

"Nothing," he finally replied to Elizabeth. "You
were just leaving, weren't you, Sawyer?"

"Sure. I just wanted to wish my successor good luck
and offer him a bit of advice."

"Whatever advice you might have is worthless. You
never bothered to follow any yourself. Now beat it, or
I'll turn you in to security."

The younger man went rigid, for a moment seem-
ing to strain against some invisible bondage. Then, as
he regained control over himself, he shot Morgan a
parting look of contempt. Lazily pushing himself from
the stable door, he wandered away.

Elizabeth wanted to question Morgan about him.
As if he sensed it, he eased away from her and went to
the stallion. Taking hold of Dancer's reins, he stroked
him reassuringly while speaking to him in a low, calm
voice. The horse sloped his ears sharply forward, listening intently and finally uttering a soft snort in reply. Elizabeth watched, mesmerized. Once again she
was reminded what a complex man he was, capable of
such diverse emotions. What magic those hands pos-

sessed. Remembering how only hours ago they'd practiced their magic on her, she felt the first sparks of arousal give rise to a blush on her cheeks. She quickly looked away—right at Spud, who was watching her sourly from beneath the crooked brim of his hat.

No, he didn't approve of her, she realized with an inner sigh, and the disappointment stung. Besides the obvious reasons, it hurt because she was aware how his opinion could affect her relationship with Morgan.

The term *relationship* caused a different type of tingling sensation to race through her. Was it a relationship or simply a fling? And was she crazy to want more than this wild, admittedly wonderful moment they were caught up in? They were so different and he'd harbored such deep resentments. That opened a potential Pandora's box of trouble, even if they hadn't had a stormy history. How could she believe she could handle all that, when she was just now letting go of her own past?

"Let's go take our seats," Morgan said, breaking into her thoughts and placing his hands lightly but possessively around her waist.

Elizabeth saw the look he exchanged with Spud and it pricked her curiosity anew. What kind of warning had that been? As he led her through the stables toward the arena entrance, she waited for a moment when they were out of earshot and asked, "What happened between you and Eddie Sawyer?"

"I fired him. I should have done it when he almost caused Kate to have a half ton of horse in her lap, but I went against my better judgment and gave him another chance. Instead of straightening up, he endangered Dancer's health, so I sent him packing."

"And now you're worried he'll do something in retaliation?"

"Not really," he replied with more confidence than he felt. "At any rate, Spud will keep an eye on things back there." He paused, wondering if he would be a fool to admit what was really bothering him. He still had difficulty in opening up to her, yet a part of him craved the intimacy true sharing brought. Would it scare her off to know his vulnerabilities? Did he want to risk everything now, when things were just beginning to improve between them?

"Morgan, you look so troubled.... Please, don't shut me out."

What the hell, he thought, steeling himself for the fall. "We need this win," he said flatly.

"Of course, you want it, but you yourself said that Zulu would have been your primary competition."

"I said we *need* it—and with or without Zulu, things can still go wrong." He knew Elizabeth couldn't understand his cryptic statements and, deciding to play for the highest stakes of his life, he drew her behind a few potted evergreens for a modicum of privacy. "Everything I have is sunk into Wildwood. Adding to that, Spud's joined me by investing his savings in the horses. I'm mortgaged up to my neck, and if we don't begin to show a profit soon... Well, you can figure it out for yourself. Without winning several championships at these kinds of events, there's no demand for our stock. It's that simple."

"It's that incredible," she countered, staring at him in disbelief. "How could you allow yourself to get into such a tight squeeze?"

Morgan told himself it was the curious glance from a passing couple that made him uncomfortable. He took hold of Elizabeth's arm. "Can we talk about this later? This isn't the time or place for this conversation."

Elizabeth wondered if it ever would be right. "I think what's bothering you is that you can't stand having your judgment criticized."

"Well, it *was* my choice to make, wasn't it?" he replied tightly.

"Thank you for pointing that out to me. The question is, why didn't you simply bet everything on the roll of a dice or a game of cards?"

"There were times when I have." At her stunned expression, he exhaled in frustration. "How do you think I earned the bulk of my money in the first place? Working as a stable hand?"

Elizabeth lowered her eyes. "Of course not, but— dear heaven! To think you could have just as easily lost . . . I can't believe you'd think any risk was worth it."

"Hell, I've been taking risks all my life. What were a few more? Besides," he added more quietly, his eyes turning haunted with the memories, "what did I have to lose after I left Meadowbrook?"

They were at their box seats and Elizabeth, conscious of her jellying legs, gratefully sat down on her chair. She was equally relieved when someone stopped by to speak to Morgan. She needed a few moments to collect herself.

Once again he'd managed to emotionally pull the rug out from under her. Granted, she'd long wondered how he'd made his fortune, and on further examination, she acknowledged she shouldn't have been surprised at what he'd told her. After all, didn't her own father harbor what he thought was a secret af-

fection for an occasional—and not inexpensive—
poker game? And weren't there a few people who believed Beaumont Center was an aging man's folly? But
the project was adequately collateralized and hardly
reflected a major percentage of her father's worth.

Morgan could lose Wildwood, and for what? To
prove yet another point?

To prove he's worthy of you.

Elizabeth jerked her head toward him. He was still
talking to the man who'd come over, which allowed
her to study him and wonder. No, she thought, it
couldn't be true. He'd already proved the only point
he'd intended to make—that he could reduce her to
putty in his hands whenever he wanted. It didn't go
any deeper than sex, at least not at this stage. Did it?

Though the man soon left, Elizabeth was relieved as
more and more people arrived and took their seats in
adjoining boxes. It canceled any further chance for
more than casual conversation.

Finally the competition began. As Elizabeth ap-
plauded the first rider entering the ring, she was aware
that, despite all the years of watching Kate compete
and agonizing with her as she worried over her up-
coming performance, she'd never been more anxious
for anyone's success than she was for Wildwood's entry.

Hours later she stood in the championship ring,
holding the silver plate Jim and Dancer's Prize had
won. She relied on her years of finishing school training and the years of experience she'd gained in apply-
ing those social skills to beam at photographers and
make small talk with well-wishers, artlessly turning the
focus of attention off herself and onto Morgan and

Wildwood Stables. Kate and Giles came by to add their congratulations. If she was disappointed that her father chose to remain invisible, she hid that, too.

Morgan stood beside her throughout. At first he was wary of the questions reporters asked, and Elizabeth could feel him stiffen beside her when one engagingly asked for the scoop on their personal relationship. She quickly tossed back a quip about neighbors having to stand together against the other solid competition that had performed.

When the crowd finally dispersed and Spud and Jim led the stallion to his trailer for the drive back to Wildwood, they found themselves alone for the first time since he'd dropped his startling news. After having hours to think of what she would say to him, Elizabeth was still confused to the point of mystification. It was a condition she suspected would be permanent for anyone who dealt with this man. But when she asked herself if she could walk away from him, the answer came back clearly and firmly. No.

"If I asked what's going on in that head of yours, would you tell me?" he inquired in a voice pitched low so only she could hear.

"I was only thinking that I'm simply, totally relieved and thrilled for you."

Unable to do more than look, he let his gaze devour her. "What would you say if I suggested we get out of here? We could go celebrate."

"That sounds nice," she murmured huskily, matching him stare for stare.

"Where would you like to go eat?"

"I'm not hungry."

"Excuse me, didn't you say—?"

"We should go celebrate." She smiled into his eyes.
"Yes."

It struck Morgan that there were only three other words that could have motivated his heart into mimicking a flying trapeze artist by launching itself up into his throat. From the moment he'd told her about his situation, he had been expecting her to make an excuse and walk out of his life. He was a man who believed in luck, but he had no faith in miracles. He was a man who believed in making the best out of a bad situation, until the opportunity arose to change it. If she had walked away, he would have been hurt, bitter and quite possibly furious enough to put his fist through the first solid object he could find. Instead, he was reduced to swallowing the lump that blocked his throat.

It was a reaction Elizabeth found endearing and it gave her reassurance. Taking his arm, she led him toward an exit. "If memory serves, I think your car is this way."

They didn't speak again until they were back on the interstate and it became obvious that they were heading toward Meadowbrook. Morgan broke the silence that had settled like morning fog between them by noting, "Our picture will be in tomorrow's paper."

"Yes."

"People will talk."

"People are already talking."

"It's only a matter of time before some enterprising reporter does his homework and discovers that I used to be your stable hand."

"My father worked in the men's clothing section of a department store when he first met my mother, who—as I'm sure you remember—was from one of the oldest families in the state. He finds it convenient to forget that, but he would be the first to say that it's what a person does with his life that's important, not where he came from.''

Morgan wished he could believe that. ''I saw him walk out when Kate and Giles came to say hello. That doesn't strike me as being an advocate of egalitarianism.''

''Wait until you're a parent and then tell me you can't understand his slip of irrationality. It's only natural that he would follow his own set of rules, when it came to obtaining what he thought was best for Kate and me.''

There was no arguing with that, but Morgan wasn't about to. He was more interested in another thought her comment had spawned. ''It's obvious you love children. Why didn't you have any of your own?''

''We'd hoped to, but Daniel—it simply didn't work out for us. I was willing to adopt. But he wanted to hold off for a while longer.'' She shook her head, not wanting to think that if she could have convinced him, at least she would have been left with someone else on whom to focus her attention.

After working at the ABA home over the past week, she'd found herself once again entertaining the idea of adopting. The laws were changing favorably for singles, and certainly being in a position to afford a child a life with all the benefits would have to work in her favor, wouldn't it?

He'd made her sad. Morgan glanced over and silently cursed himself for reminding her of the things she was missing out on. Once, during his frequent sessions of self-torment, he'd wished he *had* seduced her all those years ago. No, more than that, he wished he'd gotten her pregnant. If she'd been carrying his child, she could never have married Kirkland.

The thought that they could now be sharing a son or daughter almost ten years old was mind-blowing at first. Then subtly he felt a strange hunger gnawing at him. By the time they arrived at Wildwood, Morgan felt a cavernous hole that reached straight to his soul. It left him feeling alone, empty. It was also why, the moment he ushered Elizabeth into the house, he shut the door and immediately drew her into his arms for a kiss that was the epitome of desperation.

Empty. Yet, when Elizabeth wrapped her arms around his neck and kissed him back with equal fervor, his hollowness was filled with hope and promise. Wanting it, wanting *her* as he'd never wanted in his life, he lifted her into his arms and started up the stairs.

"Morgan..." Elizabeth didn't know whether to laugh or cover her eyes against the dizzy whirl. "I could walk."

He paused on the third stair. "Spud has free run of the house. Do you want to have him wander in and find us making love right here? Because that's where it's going to happen, if I don't get you up to my room in the next thirty seconds."

If she thought he was teasing, she had only to examine the taut planes of his face and the fierce, primordial look in his eyes to know he was dead serious. As he took the silver plate that was caught between them and tossed it like a Frisbee onto the couch across the room, hot bubbles of excitement scampered through her body. And when he reached his bedroom, kicked the door closed and locked it, she clung to him, certain that if he released her, she would melt into a small puddle at his feet.

She needn't have worried. He wasn't about to let go. Pressing her back against the door, sandwiching her between it and his powerful body, he reinitiated the kiss he'd begun downstairs.

No one, no one would ever take her from tranquility to a high fever with a kiss and touch as he would, she thought, plowing her hands into his hair to insure she got all the heat he had to offer her. She might not recognize herself with him, but it was only with him that she felt fully alive.

"Too many damned clothes," he muttered, trying to strip off her jacket, just as she was tugging his from his shoulders. Trapped in their makeshift straitjackets, their eyes met and something between frustration and humor transmitted itself on the shallow breaths that wafted between them. Morgan lowered his forehead to hers. "One of us has to be patient."

"I hope you're not looking for volunteers?"

Without blinking, Morgan took a step back. "What if I suggested that every man—" he shrugged out of his jacket and, in another spare move, whipped his turtleneck over his head "—and woman fend for themselves?"

His broad shoulders were muscular from strenuous labor, and there wasn't an ounce of fat on his rib cage. The memory of how his firm chest and taut abdomen had quivered under the exploration of her fingers had a slow smile curving her lips. They might be older and hopefully wiser than they had been ten years ago, but he still could no more keep his hands off her than she could keep hers off him, and she intended to prove it.

"You mean like this?" she asked innocently, letting her own jacket drop away. Then, hardly missing a beat, she reached behind her to unzip her skirt and let it slide over her hips to the floor.

She wasn't wearing a slip beneath the suede skirt, and the possessive gleam in Morgan's narrow-eyed stare was as physically exciting as a caress. He took in her knee-high, suede boots, the sheer hose secured by a white, lace-trimmed garter, her silk blouse that offered the hint of finer lingerie beneath it, and exhaled heavily.

"Yeah," he murmured gruffly, wondering how she'd managed to outshine his fantasies. Before she could even begin to unbutton her blouse, he closed the distance between them and, sweeping one arm around her waist, drew her tightly against him. "But on second thought," he said, gliding his hand down the back of her right leg to release a garter, "let me help."

One by one he released the others, leaving her skin tingling wherever he touched her, until she forgot all about what she'd been doing and wanted to do and sought a mind-drugging kiss. Within seconds the playfulness and teasing were gone, replaced by greedy touches and deep-throated moans. No, there was no fighting this need, she thought. As he lifted her, she eagerly wrapped her legs around his waist and let him carry her to his bed.

They fell in a tangle, barely catching their breath before seeking each other's mouths again. Hands fumbled blindly with the remainder of their clothing until, completely naked, Morgan slid down to take her breast into his mouth. His teeth and tongue were merciless. So were hers as she nipped his shoulder, the side of his neck, his ear.

"One of these days," he rasped as she succeeded in making him shudder again, "we're going to take this slow and easy."

"But not today," Elizabeth replied just as breathlessly.

"No." He parted her legs and probed the moist heat he craved to lose himself in. "Not—oh, damn."

Remembering his responsibility to protect them, he began to pull away and reach for his drawer. Elizabeth stopped him. "Don't ruin this. It's too perfect."

Her words, the entreaty behind them, sent white-hot flames searing through him. As she coaxed him back, he knew he should resist, but instead crushed her deeper into the bedding. "Elizabeth—*think*."

"No." She closed her eyes because she didn't want to think, didn't want to explain. Most of all, she didn't want to know if he disapproved or would refuse her. She simply wanted him. All of him. "Please."

"Damn—" Before he could decide, she was taking him, and he had to clutch at the bedding at either side of her head to keep from giving in to mindless pleasure and driving deeper. "Elizabeth, damn it, look at me," he growled.

Slowly she opened her eyes. In the depths of his she saw herself, the same awareness of how their bodies were already pulsating, and that he wanted this as desperately as she did.

"If you become— If it happens," he rasped, unable to keep from giving in to the natural rhythm that called to him.

"It probably won't. I think it's the wrong time."

"But if it does—"

"I wouldn't hold you responsible."

He swore, furious because she was resisting him, even as she sweetly sapped his strength. The words wouldn't come. But they were etched on his heart. *If it happened, they would make this legal. His child wouldn't be born a bastard. If it happened . . . if it happened.*

As he felt himself hurled toward fulfillment, he crushed his mouth to hers, the whisper a prayer in his mind. *Please, God, let it happen.*

Nine

Morgan stood in the doorway of the stables and watched dusk overtake the landscape. A solitary star flickered above the horizon like a diamond on dusky velvet. It looked cold and lonely, exactly the way he felt. The former condition he could fix if he went into the house, instead of standing there jacketless. The latter would take a lot more to cure.

"It's gonna rain," Spud said, coming from the tack room and alternately massaging his stiff leg and his arthritic shoulder. "Always know when it's gonna rain and when it's gonna get cold."

"Mmm."

He gave Morgan's back a sidelong look. "Only thing an old body is good for."

"Mmm-hmm."

"I ought to get an extra cut of the profits for being the resident barometer."

"Hmm."

Spud swore and pushed his hat off his forehead. "If you think you're going to mope around here like a lovesick hound for the rest of the evening, you've got another think coming. Yesterday was bad enough."

"What are you talking about?" Morgan demanded, scowling over his shoulder at the other man.

"You know damn well. It's that Beaumont woman."

"Her name's Elizabeth."

"Her name's trouble," Spud muttered, easing up beside him and brushing lingering straw and dust from his coveralls. "She's got you tied in such a knot, you'd give a pretzel twister crossed eyes."

Because he was right, Morgan hooked his thumbs into the loops of his jeans and glared back at him. "Is there something in particular you want to complain about? Did I leave one of the corral gates open? Did I neglect to hang some tack where it belongs? Did I inadvertently breathe in your airspace?"

"Aha! See there? You don't hear from her for a measly two days and you're ready to snap my head off."

What he was, Morgan thought, was ready to crawl the walls. Not because he hadn't spoken to Elizabeth since he'd taken her home Saturday night, because he had. He'd phoned her yesterday and had asked her to have dinner with him. But she'd had to decline because she was hostessing a dinner party for her father, who was entertaining some business associates. Today her excuse had been just as legitimate; she was working at the ABA children's home and—since Giles was out of town—Kate was coming over for dinner and to spend the night. She'd agreed to see him tomorrow, and just thinking of the soft, husky yes she'd given sent ripples of hot pleasure through him.

Realistically Morgan knew he should be content; realistically he knew that it would be sensible to take some time to get used to the idea of them being together. There was still so much they didn't know about each other, there were so many years of anger to make up for. But he wasn't the kind of man to settle for contentment and he was hardly in the mood to be patient. Not after what they'd shared last night.

If their first time together had changed him, yesterday had convinced him; they belonged together. Why waste precious time tiptoeing around the truth, when they could be spending it far more satisfyingly? How much time did they have, at best another fifty or sixty years?

"You should see your face," Spud mumbled, disgusted. "I haven't seen anything so lovesick since Dancer took a fancy to his first mare."

"Go to hell."

Morgan took a step into the spreading darkness, as much to avoid Spud's unwelcome but keen perception as to invite the cold air to soothe the rising heat in his body. All that happened was that he felt loneliness settle into his weary bones like the debilitating ache caused by autumn dampness.

Lovesickness. That was his ailment, all right. He was tired of being alone, of being bitter and of shutting himself off from the warmth love offered. He, who'd believed he would never risk the vulnerability of opening himself to another living soul, had fallen like a ton of granite breaking off Stone Mountain and crashing to the earth. All it had taken was a certain, liquid-voiced woman whispering, *"It's too perfect."*

"Aw—why don't you get out of here," Spud said, gesturing toward the pickup. "Any fool can see it's terminal. Nothing more pitiful than witnessing a man dangling like a hooked fish. Go get her."

As tempted as he was, Morgan shook his head. "It's not that easy. For one thing, her father disapproves of me."

"If they ever take a survey, they'll probably come up with the unsurprising news that most fathers ain't too fond of the men their daughters end up with. He'll either change his mind or get used to the idea. Don't matter none, anyway, since it ain't him you're sleeping with."

"You don't know Elizabeth," Morgan replied, though he felt he was arguing with himself more than Spud. "She married Kirkland to please her father. How am I supposed to fight her sense of family responsibility?"

"She didn't look like she was putting up much of a battle the other day at the horse show."

"Would you give her a break? If it wasn't for her, we would've been a three-line mention in the paper. Whose influence do you think got us on the six o'clock news?"

"Now you're making her the patron saint of struggling horse breeders."

Morgan spun around and glared at the man who resembled a grimacing elf. "No, damn it, I'm just saying that she doesn't deserve to be grouped in the same category as your ex-wives."

"Course not. My exes weren't that good-looking!" Spud snapped back.

If he hadn't felt so lousy, Morgan would have smiled. Not one to make overt gestures or to apologize, he surprised Spud by closing the distance between them and gripping his friend's shoulder. "I'm sorry.... I know I've been a pain lately."

"Yeah. If I wanted to be nagged all the time, I'd have stayed married." Spud mimicked a quick, one-two punch to Morgan's abdomen. But just as abruptly he grew serious. "You want her? Go after her. Me, I'm hungry. I'm going to go see what's in the refrigerator. You want me to fix you something, too?"

"No," Morgan replied, a determined expression settling over his face. "I think I'll take care of it myself."

"This is nice," Teddy said, beaming across the table at one daughter and then the other. "Just like old times, eh, girls? I know you miss Giles, Kate, but you have to admit that it's good to have a family to come home to, isn't it?"

"Yes, Daddy. Liz, if you're not going to eat your stuffed brioche, can I have it?"

Elizabeth, pursing her lips to hide her smile, passed her appetizer plate to her sister. "Just like old times, all right. After all these years, you'd think Leona would know to make double portions of everything for you."

"I'm practicing for when I have to eat for two."

Teddy almost choked on his burgundy. As he pressed his linen napkin to his mouth, he eyed his younger daughter through tearing eyes. "You're barely two months married. What are you talking about?"

Guileless blue eyes blinked back at him. "Well, gee, Daddy...how long does it take?"

As their father muttered about proper conversation around a dinner table, Elizabeth adjusted the napkin in her lap and took a sip of her own wine. How long, indeed? she wondered, thinking of the potential repercussions of her impulsive behavior with Morgan. All day, while playing with the children at the ABA home, she'd debated over the idea of taking a detour on the way home and buying one of those home pregnancy kits. Of course, it would have been a waste of money. Hadn't she'd awakened to a sore back and tender breasts, her normal signal that her cycle was only days away? But it had been wonderful to daydream. Hope.

She wondered if Morgan was feeling anything similar. He'd said all the right things that night, hadn't he? And there'd been such intensity in his voice, his eyes. Yet when she'd told him she'd be tied up on Sunday and couldn't see him today, he hadn't seemed overly disappointed.

"Liz? Liz!" Kate tilted her head inquiringly at her sister. "Are you all right?"

"Yes—why do you ask?"

"Oh, no special reason. I simply asked you how your day at the home went—twice—and you looked through me like I was a piece of cellophane."

"Did I? I'm sorry." Elizabeth took another sip of her wine and silently warned herself to be more careful around her sister. *No one* was better at scenting things than Kate. "I suppose I was still thinking about one of the children at the home," she said truthfully, since after thoughts of Morgan, little Rebecca had been a major concern. "Do you remember the child I mentioned, whose mother was in an alcohol recovery program? Well, Rebecca was supposed to be reunited with her this week, but the woman suffered a set-back."

"Oh—the poor kid. She must be devastated."

"Crushed. We spent hours in her closet."

"What do you mean 'we'?" Teddy asked, trying to follow the conversation. "You literally crawled into a closet with her?"

Elizabeth toyed with the remaining silverware beside her plate. "When Rebecca feels like everything in her world is coming apart or turning against her, she hides in the closet in her bedroom."

Kate leaned toward Teddy. "She's being generous with her description. The things are about the size of a matchbox. The rooms themselves aren't much bigger. In fact the next time you're looking for a charity, Daddy, call me. I'd like to give you a guided tour of a worthy recipient."

With a dramatic sigh, Teddy laid his own appetizer fork on his plate. "How is it that you can turn the simplest inquiries into a bid for a donation?"

Reaching over to pat his hand, Kate turned back to Elizabeth. "Was she feeling better when you left?"

"She agreed to go in to dinner. I suppose I should take heart in that. But—is it normal to feel so helpless?"

"Mmm-hmm. No matter how much you do, all you'll ever see is how much more there is that needs to be done. However," Kate added with a warm smile, "I have to tell you that I've never been more proud of you."

Leona came in from the kitchen, wheeling the dinner cart and humming under her breath. One by one she took away the first-course dishes and replaced them with the main course.

"Prime rib! You angel!" Kate cried, eagerly eyeing the fare. "You must have been reading my mind. Giles is on a fish kick lately, and I swear I've been having dreams about pulling into the nearest drive-thru restaurant and ordering a double cheeseburger."

"Well, there's plenty more in the kitchen for you if you want it," Leona assured her. She circled to Elizabeth's side of the table and eyed her empty plate. "Now that's what I like to see. About time you ate more than two bites of this and one of that and put a little meat back on them bones."

"It was delicious, Leona, thank you," Elizabeth said, keeping her eyes on the amber-hued arrangement of chrysanthemums and carnations in the center of the table.

"You don't think I put too much garlic or paprika in it, do you?"

"Er, no. It was just right."

"Uh-huh." Leona exchanged the empty plate with one laden with a thick slice of juicy beef and vegetables. "Wasn't any of either in it, but you'd have known that if'n you ate it, missy. Now I expect you to do justice to this, or you'll get the biggest piece of cheesecake. Hear?"

Elizabeth stared down at the pink, juice-flowing slice of meat. "Leona—this thing still has a heartbeat. You know I like my food more well-done."

"When them boys in those think tanks figure out a way to cook each slice of meat to please everybody around a dinner table, we'll talk about it. In the meantime, your daddy likes his rare, Miss Kate likes hers rare—so you gotta be happy with the end cut. It's the best I can do." At Elizabeth's mournful expression she sighed. "Want me to turn it over so you don't have to look at the blood?"

"*Leona.* Is it absolutely necessary—?" The sound of the doorbell had everyone in the room exchanging questioning glances. As Leona went to investigate, Elizabeth called after her. "Whoever it is, invite them for dinner. They can have mine."

"You don't suppose Giles got back early, do you?" Teddy asked Kate.

She shook her head. "He would have phoned first. Anyway, I told him that the painters wouldn't be finished with the bedrooms and that the house would be in a shambles for another few days, so if he had business to take care of, now was as good a time as any to be away from home. Of course, if he's gone more than another day, I'm going to hop on a plane and go after him," she added, wiggling her eyebrows.

"Poor Giles," Elizabeth drawled. "The man's going to be gray before he's forty."

Teddy pretended to have something caught in his throat, but failing to hide his amusement, took another sip of his wine.

"Speaking of irresistible men," Kate said with a sly gleam in her eye. "What's new with you and—?"

"I won't have that man discussed at the dinner table," Teddy declared, his mood shifting abruptly. He ignored the wide-eyed looks both women sent him and viciously cut into his prime rib.

Kate recovered first and rolled her eyes in exasperation. "Daddy, really. You can be such a snobby old grouch."

He sat back in his captain's chair, his expression openly wounded. "I am *not* a snob. I'm a father who's concerned about the future welfare of his children and, as such, I do not condone any self-respecting daughter of mine to be flagrantly cavorting with an irreverent renegade like Deveroux.''

"There was a time when people called you similar things, Father. Yes, we've heard them," Elizabeth said quietly at his startled look. "The girls at school enjoyed repeating what they'd overheard from their parents' conversations."

"My favorite was Beaumont the Buccaneer," Kate added cheerfully.

"What I'm trying to say," Elizabeth said, shooting her sister a speaking glance, "is that you of all people should understand what he went through to succeed in his business."

Teddy laid down his fork and sat up straighter in his chair. "I may not have been born a gentleman, but I know how to conduct myself as one. Deveroux doesn't give a damn. Why, do you know I heard that when he was in Kentucky there was this wife of a judge—"

"Ahem." At the other end of the room Leona cleared her throat and stepped aside to let their visitor enter. "The renegade's here to see Miss Elizabeth."

As she disappeared into the kitchen, Morgan grimly took note of the embarrassed faces around the table and stiffly inclined his head. "Obviously the old saying about one never hearing good behind one's back is true. Excuse me for interrupting," he said, turning to leave.

Elizabeth dropped her fork onto her plate and jumped to her feet. "Morgan, wait!"

"Sit down," Teddy commanded.

She ignored him and hurried around the table. Taking Morgan's hand in both of hers, she coaxed him back into the room. "Come in. Join us."

How did she keep getting lovelier? Morgan thought, unable to make his feet follow his brain's message. Her hair was swept behind one ear, and in the soft chandelier light it looked like a halo of spun gold; her silvery-blue knit dress gently outlined slender curves he'd dreamt of in his sleep.... "Do you really think that's a good idea?" he asked quietly, his eyes warming with feelings he could no longer keep hidden from her. "I didn't come to create problems for you with your family."

She lowered her eyes to the hand she held. "Tell me why you *did* come," she asked, just as softly.

"You know."

"Tell me."

"I couldn't stay away."

Her smile came like a blossom unfolding after a spring rain, and she shifted her hold so she could take his arm. Turning, she looked at her father, who sat scowling forbiddingly at the head of the table. "Dad—"

He pointed a finger in warning. "Elizabeth—don't you dare."

Gripping Morgan's arm more tightly, she replied with quiet dignity, "All my life I've tried to be the model of perfection for you, Dad. After Mother died, the very thought of seeing you grieving or disappointed was something I wanted to avoid at all costs, so I was always careful to follow the rules. I even married the man I knew you'd secretly chosen for me. I never caused you a moment's worry, did I?"

"Because that's who you are!" Teddy declared, firmly slapping down his palm on the linen-covered table. Just as abruptly his expression grew wheedling.

"Elizabeth...Princess, it isn't like you to question my better judgment."

"I'm not your little girl anymore, Dad. I have to follow my own mind and my own heart. It would please me to know you understood and accepted that—and invited Morgan to join us."

Teddy's bushy eyebrows shot upward. "What— that, too?"

Before anyone could say anything else, there was a commotion in the kitchen and Jackson burst through the swinging door. Leona was right behind him, scolding him about tracking mud through her clean house. Jackson spotted Morgan and, gasping to catch his breath, pointed in the direction from which he'd come.

"You'd better get back. The sky over Wildwood's as bright as day. Fire—it has to be."

Morgan strode to the dining-room window and drew back the heavy draperies. Just as Jackson had said, the eastern sky was a bright, unnatural orange. "The horses," he whispered, bolting for the door.

"I'm coming with you," Elizabeth told him, right on his heels.

"Call the fire department and get the hands!" Teddy ordered Jackson. "Elizabeth! Wait! Damn— Jackson, pick me up out front."

"We can take my car," Kate said, already heading for the same door Elizabeth and Morgan had disappeared through.

It took less than five minutes to cover the distance from Meadowbrook to Wildwood. During that time Morgan didn't say a word to Elizabeth. Because she was certain their thoughts and fears ran parallel, she chose not to break the silence. She, too, wondered how

bad it was . . . worried if the animals were trapped. . . .
Were Spud, Miguel and Jimmy all right?

A fire truck was pulling into the driveway, just as
Morgan turned the last bend. Another could be spotted farther down the road. They were the only two
trucks in the volunteer unit, and judging from the
flames rising above both the pecan orchard and the
hill, Morgan knew that wasn't going to be enough.

Downshifting, he gunned the truck up the hill. Even
though prepared for the worst, he was stunned when
he saw the main house engulfed in flames.

"Oh, Lord," Elizabeth whispered.

Morgan made a sharp right and parked the truck
between two trees, well out of the way of danger and
traffic. Though they were several hundred feet from
the house, the moment he got out of the truck he could
feel the heat of the fire on his face and hands, hear the
blood-chilling sound of animals' shrill screams of terror. Accepting that the house was a loss, he yelled to
Elizabeth to stay put and took off for the stables.

Elizabeth never considered it for a moment. Ludi-
crous though it was to think she could keep up with
him in her high heels, she followed as quickly as she
was able.

Circling trucks, dodging men and sprinting over
water hoses, Morgan saw Miguel trying to lead a wild-
eyed Lady Gray from the stables. "Let her run for the
woods!" he shouted above the roar of the flames.
"Let her go!"

Miguel did, giving the mare an added slap on her
rump. He immediately headed back inside for another horse. At first Morgan thought the stables were
burning, too, but he was relieved to discover it was
simply smoke from the house that was spreading into

the barn. "Where's Spud?" he shouted, having spotted Jimmy, who appeared unhurt and was leading out another mare. Before Miguel could answer, Morgan heard another high-pitched scream. Ducking to peer beneath the thinner smoke, he saw Spud desperately trying to get Dancer's Prize out of his stall. The stallion, wild with fear, was determined to kick anyone who got near him.

Racing to them, Morgan not only grabbed the reins from Spud, but caught the older man just as he began to slump to the ground. There was a gash on his friend's right temple, and blood ran down the side of his face. "Hang on, I'm going to get you outside."

"Dancer...take Dancer."

"I've got him, too."

"Can't manage both of us."

"Let me help," Elizabeth said, coming up on Spud's other side and slipping her arms around his thick waist.

"I told you to stay put!" Morgan shouted, before breaking into a racking cough.

She matched him glare for glare. "Are we all going to get asphyxiated or get out of here?" Without waiting for a reply, she began to lead Spud outside and away from the worst of the smoke. A fire fighter spotted them and came to offer assistance.

After they settled Spud on one of the wrought iron benches circling an old oak, the fire fighter gestured back to his truck. "That gash looks nasty. Let me get the first aid kit. We've contacted another station, and they should be bringing an ambulance in a few minutes."

"Don't need any ambulance," Spud muttered thickly.

Elizabeth sat down beside him, using her body to keep him from tipping over. Blood from his wound was beginning to run into his eyes. Without hesitation she untied the loose knot on the silk scarf around her neck and gently wiped away what she could.

"Hey—are you crazy? You'll ruin that thing."

"It doesn't matter."

"Hmph...I guess not. You can always buy another one, can't you."

Ignoring the disappointment his censure caused, Elizabeth lightly pressed the scarf to his wound. "Does that hurt?"

"Everything hurts. Let someone smack *you* over the head with a crowbar, and tell me how you feel."

Elizabeth's heart plummeted. "Who, Spud? Who did this to you?"

"Sawyer. He must have been hiding in the woods, even before Morgan left. I caught him pouring gasoline inside. Getting even, he said. Crazy fool's what I say. I knew I couldn't stop him, so I took off to get Miguel and Jimmy, but he caught up with me out back. Next thing I knew, the house was a flaming torch and Jim was dragging me away from it."

"Where's Eddie now?" Elizabeth asked, glancing back at the inferno that was devouring the lovely old house. But she wasn't really sure she wanted to know. The thought of coming face-to-face with someone who was capable of something like this made her stomach queasy.

"They got him. Knocked him out good and got him trussed up like a Christmas goose over by the corral. Going to hand him over to the sheriff—that is, if there's anything left of him, once Morgan finds out what happened."

"Oh, Lord...we've got to keep Morgan away from him, Spud."

"Lady, do you realize that lunatic would have fried Morgan, too, if he'd had the chance?"

"And do you realize that Morgan could go to jail himself, if he tries to take justice into his own hands?"

The panic in her voice must have reached through Spud's anger and pain. Inching his head to an angle where he could look at her through his good eye, he considered her for a long moment. "I was worried that this was all one-sided between you two, but it's not, is it?"

Elizabeth had to look away because of the sudden tears that burned in her eyes. "I understand. That's why you'd decided not to like me. Well, if it's any consolation—no, it's definitely not one-sided."

The fireman returned, putting an abrupt end to that subject. As he began to attend to Spud, Kate and Teddy arrived. Elizabeth, intent on finding Morgan before he found Eddie, asked her to stay with Spud. Then she turned to her father.

"Dad, I might need your help. Could you come with me?"

With a nod, Teddy took his suit jacket off and put it around her shoulders, then followed her toward the barn and corrals. As they went, they kept glancing over at the blaze and the men fighting it. They, too, understood that it was a losing battle.

"You don't think about how it can all be gone so quickly," Teddy mused. "You work, struggle for years and then within minutes—"

"I know." Elizabeth hugged his arm. "But we can't think about that right now. What's most important is finding Morgan." Quickly she told him what Spud had relayed to her and what she herself knew about Eddie Sawyer. "If Morgan gets to him before we can stop him, I don't know what he's liable to do, Dad."

As they'd feared, upon approaching the corrals they saw that Morgan had gotten the last of the horses out and that Miguel and Jimmy were trying desperately to keep him from Eddie. In the meantime, Eddie had regained consciousness and was taunting Morgan.

Elizabeth ran the rest of the way and wrapped her arms around Morgan's waist. "Listen to me. Let the sheriff handle this. Don't you see? He wants you to get into trouble."

"He won't be disappointed. Damn it, Miguel, stand back or I'll fire you. You, too, Jim."

"Don't let go, and we'll guarantee you jobs at Meadowbrook with a ten percent raise. Right, Dad?"

Teddy winced. "*Ten?* Er, oh, all right."

Frustrated, Morgan tried to jerk free, then turned his fierce gaze upon the man who only a half hour ago had all but ordered him out of his home. "What's it to you if I get arrested for giving him what he deserves? Isn't that just the kind of thing you'd like to see happen to get rid of me?"

"Now you're talking as crazy as he is," Teddy replied, gesturing to Eddie. "I might not like this idea my girl's got in her head about you, but I'm smart enough not to test her on it. You want to lose her, you do it without my help. In the meantime calm down and concentrate on saving your stock. Let the law take care of the rest. Believe me, I'll see this boy is locked away for a long time."

Elizabeth watched Morgan's face. Slowly he closed his eyes, and just as slowly she felt the anger drain out of him. She might have been relieved, only she understood better than anyone that it wasn't over. She wouldn't have been able to describe what she'd seen in his eyes seconds ago, but she had the strangest feeling that a door had slammed somewhere inside him...and that, worst of all, she'd been locked out, on the other side.

Hours later, Elizabeth drove Morgan to Meadowbrook. The fire was out. Spud was in the hospital for overnight observation, and Miguel and Jimmy were staying with the horses. It had taken quite a bit of coaxing, but she'd finally convinced him that a few hours' rest away from Wildwood were the best thing for him at the moment.

Teddy had returned with Kate earlier, but was still up and in his study. As they entered the foyer, he came to meet them at the stairs. Not one to mince words, he immediately asked if there was hope of anything being salvageable.

"Do you think anything could be left after an inferno like that?" Morgan asked, his voice raw from smoke and fatigue.

"Then you'll rebuild. It'll be inconvenient, of course—"

"No, there won't be any rebuilding."

"What are you talking about? After the insurance company pays your claim, you'll have every contractor in the area vying for the job to rebuild the house."

Morgan gripped the handrail and stared at the red and amber design in the carpet at his feet. "They'll be wasting their breath, since I only carried the minimum requirement of insurance on the house and nothing for its contents. Whatever I get from the claim, I'll need it to keep the business going."

"I see." Teddy stroked his whiskery jaw. "Well...maybe we can work around that. As I see it, I owe you an apology for my earlier behavior.... How about if I loan you the money until you're back on your feet?"

It was all Morgan could do not to turn around and walk out of the house. He was so tired. Still, he met Teddy's inquiring gaze with determination. "Fourteen years ago you gave a drifter a job. I'll always be grateful to you for that, but I'll be damned if I'm going back to old patterns. Thanks, but no thanks."

He started up the stairs. Elizabeth signaled to her father not to say anything else and hurried after him. She showed Morgan to the room beside hers and even remained calm when she understood the brief thanks he tossed over his shoulder were a dismissal. Without comment, she turned and shut the door.

Morgan slowly released his breath then swung around to set the lock. He froze as he caught sight of Elizabeth.

"Do you think I'm going to be that easy to get rid of?" she asked conversationally.

He clenched the hands at his sides into fists. "Let's not drag this out, Elizabeth. I appreciate all you've done and I appreciate the room, but if you don't get out of here, you'll leave me with no choice but to head back to my place to sleep on a few bales of hay."

"I have your truck keys, remember?" She lifted a finely arched brow suggestively. "Of course, I wouldn't deny you your right to search me for them."

Morgan couldn't keep himself from sweeping his gaze downward over her body, and he couldn't stop the ache that sprang to life when he thought of all the years of emptiness he had to look forward to; but when he spoke, he almost succeeded in keeping his voice cool. "You don't get it yet, do you? Well, let me spell it out for you. It's over. I give up...you...the ambitions to have my own place...everything. In fact, you can forget what I said about using the insurance money to keep the business going. I'm going to return Spud's investment and use the rest to get as far away from this place as I can."

"That's exhaustion talking. Tomorrow—"

"Tomorrow I'll see that it's the first smart thought I've had in years. I must have been nuts to think I could ever pull this off."

Fear crept up Elizabeth's throat, but she ignored it and raised her chin. "You won't walk away from me."

"I told you before that I had no use for spoiled, rich girls."

"You managed to come up with a few in the last few days."

Unbidden, the memories of making love to her flooded Morgan's mind and shot his body temperature up several degrees. He swore silently. "It's not going to work, honey. Now scram. I've got just enough patience left to end this without destroying the few good memories we have. At least let me leave with them intact."

Ignoring him, Elizabeth pursed her lips. "You know, people are really beginning to respect you around here. Why throw it away? I know—" she added quickly before he could reply. "You don't have enough capital, and you won't take a loan from my father."

"Bingo. End of conversation."

"Not quite," she replied, dropping her gaze, but watching him from beneath her thick lashes. "I have another suggestion, Morgan. I have my own money. Borrow it from me."

Ten

Waging one battle against despair and another against violence, Morgan took a step toward her. "Lady, don't push your luck."

Elizabeth nodded sympathetically. "It's a shock, I know. You're thinking about your sense of pride. I understand all about pride, remember? There've been times when I felt I had too much of it myself. But think about it, Morgan. It's not as if we both wouldn't be benefiting from this."

"And how do you figure that?" he found himself asking despite his better judgment.

Though she'd never been more serious in her life, she strove to keep her tone whimsical and her expression flirtatious. "Why, you didn't think this would be interest free, did you? And I suppose I should warn you that my rates are high—I want at least two children. Maybe three, if we hurry." She affected a calm shrug and turned to grip the doorknob. "You probably need a few hours to think about it. Sleep well. You can give me your answer in the morning."

Before she could get the door open more than six inches, Morgan had crossed the room. He slammed the door shut with a force that shook the dresser mirror.

"Morgan!" Elizabeth scolded in a loud whisper. "There are people trying to sleep in this house."

"I don't give a damn if we wake up the entire county. What the hell do you think you're doing?"

Elizabeth stared at the panel design and concentrated on keeping her nervousness out of her voice. "I thought that was obvious."

His palm flat against the door, his body nearly aligned with hers, Morgan found himself breathing like Dancer after a full workout, and it didn't help that with each breath he took, he could still smell the fresh scent of her shampoo beneath the odor of smoke. "You're nuts," he growled.

Taking full advantage of their proximity, Elizabeth slowly turned, letting her body stroke against his like a preening cat. "I know. You're thinking about the problem this presents. You're wondering what people will say, what they'll think. But the way I look at it, who cares? There'll always be someone out there who'll doubt your motives and call you an opportunist." She reached up to stroke an ash smudge from his cheek. "The challenge will be to prove them wrong."

Morgan knew every second he spent standing there, listening to her sweet foolishness, was one in which he was losing his resistance. He should have put her out of the room five minutes ago and bolted the door to keep her out. Furious with them both, he grasped her upper arms and pulled her closer against him. "Stop it! Do you think this is some kind of game?"

"Not at all," Elizabeth said, her heart in her eyes. "But I don't know how else to tell you that I won't let you go without a fight."

"It wouldn't work. We're too different. Once the novelty wore off, you'd be miserable. Your father was right—I am a renegade. I don't think I'd know how to do anything the easy way, even if I had the means."

"In case you haven't noticed, this family thrives on renegades."

"Elizabeth—"

"No!" She closed her eyes, afraid of the rejection she might see in his. "Listen to me, Morgan. Neither of us knows what tomorrow will bring, and I can't make a naive promise that I'm going to adore every venture you decide to get involved with. But what I *do* know is that we share something deep and special that deserves a chance. The question is—do you think you could learn to love me enough to give it a try?"

"I don't have to try," he said, his voice not quite steady. "I already love you too much. I'll be loving you until they plant me in the ground." Unable to find other words he covered her mouth with his.

There was a tender ferocity in his first kiss, for having previously resigned himself to the necessity of giving her up, he had to reassure himself that she wasn't a dream that would evaporate at his touch.

His passion thrilled Elizabeth, just as his tenderness made her want to weep. She drew back her head and, teary-eyed, gazed up at him.

"In case you're interested, I love you, too."

He knew she wanted him to smile, but he wasn't quite ready yet. "You're going to have to remind me once in a while," he whispered, stroking her soft skin with the backs of his fingers and spreading kisses from her lips to her forehead and back to her chin. "I don't have a lot of experience with miracles." Growing even more serious, he framed her face with his hands. "Are you sure this is what you want? You deserve so much more."

"I love you. I think I've been fighting it since I was sixteen. It was—you were so overwhelming. No more, Morgan. I think this is our time at last." Mischief sparkled in her eyes and she wedged her hand between them. "You want to shake so we have a legitimate deal?"

The slow, predatory smile she adored spread over his face and, ignoring her hand, he swept her up and into his arms. "I have a better idea how to seal a contract."

Elizabeth thought he was going to place her on the bed, but as he headed for the bathroom, she broke into laughter. "Morgan, what are you doing?"

"Well, we're both sooty. What do you think Leona's going to say if she finds the bed sheets covered with the stuff in the morning—including both pillowcases?"

"Not quite as much as my father will say, when he discovers that my bed hasn't been slept in."

In the bathroom Morgan placed her on the oval rug outside the shower stall. After reaching inside the stall to turn on both taps, he occupied his not quite steady hands with unbuttoning the pearl studs on her dress, while Elizabeth busied herself with unfastening his shirt and tugging it out of his jeans. Suddenly the humor that had made them laugh seconds ago was being replaced with an emotion far more poignant.

"Make sure this is what you want," he told her as he bared her subtle curves to his hands and lips. "Because once you have my ring on your finger, I'll never let you go."

"It goes both ways," she murmured, parting the shirt she'd unbuttoned to place a kiss over his heart.

Morgan buried his hands deep in her hair and encouraged her to repeat the caress. "You owned my heart the first time I laid eyes on you."

"Really?" A teasing smile curved her lips as she gently nipped him with her teeth. "And what was that bit of gossip my father wanted to share with me regarding a certain judge's wife?"

Morgan lifted her face to his. "Exactly what you said—gossip. She was a bored lady who thought that a few invitations and words of support to her Kentucky society friends obligated me to providing her with an invitation to my bed. When I disagreed, she alluded to our having an affair, anyway, because it stroked her ego."

"Her husband couldn't have been thrilled."

"Her husband was having an affair with one of his clerks and thought I was doing him a favor. He offered to put in a good word for me with his own circle of friends, if I'd keep his wife happy." As Elizabeth mastered his belt buckle and drew down the zipper on his jeans, her knuckles lightly caressed him, causing him to suck in his breath. "Can we change the subject? This isn't exactly what I want to talk about."

Morgan eased the last scrap of silk she was wearing over her hips, then languidly stroked the smoother skin he'd uncovered, until Elizabeth pressed closer to him in search of more. "What do you want to talk about?" she asked throatily.

"How about telling me you love me again? I don't think I could ever hear that enough, especially—Elizabeth!" He grabbed her wrist. "Damn, let me get out of the rest of these clothes. Ah . . . Elizabeth."

She smiled against his chest. "I love the way you say my name. . . . I love the way you feel. . . . I love *you*, Morgan."

"I hope these walls are thick," he muttered, wrapping an arm around her waist and taking her with him beneath the shower's brisk spray. "Because I think we're in for another long night."

Elizabeth laughed again, then sighed with pleasure as Morgan claimed her lips for a long, fulfilling kiss.

Minutes later Kate smiled as she passed their door. Securing the tie of her pale blue satin robe, she descended the staircase. A light was on in her father's study and, peeking inside, she found him pacing, a brooding frown furrowing his brow.

"Looks like I'm not the only one who can't sleep," she said, stepping into the room. "I was going to go into the kitchen and make some hot chocolate. Care to join me?"

"Might as well. Confounded, stubborn man has me all wound up."

"We're speaking of Morgan, I presume?"

"Who else? The man says he won't be able to afford to replace his home, but when I offer to make him a loan, he turns down that, as well. Is that crazy or what?"

"Well, you know Morgan, Daddy. He has his own principles." She turned to go to the kitchen. "Be back in a minute with that hot chocolate."

Hardly paying attention, Teddy returned to his pacing. "I'll win yet. Just see if I don't."

Having decided this conversation was too interesting to cut short, Kate retraced her steps from the door. "Wait a minute. Since when did this turn into a contest of wills?"

Teddy ignored that, too, and continued to plot. "I'll make him an offer he can't refuse. What do you think of this? I'll give him half of Meadowbrook as a wedding present. We could take down the fence between our lands. Think of it.... We'll be bigger and stronger than ever. He won't have time to handle all the business that comes his way. And you know, I had another idea.... In Kentucky he was considering getting into the racing business."

"How do you know that?"

"I have my sources. Anyway, we could do that here. We'll need a track. Maybe even—"

"Hold on a minute," Kate said, playfully indignant. "Do you realize you're bartering away half of my inheritance?"

"What do you need it for? You moved into that cave you bought from that crazy artist. Besides, you have your trust and Channing. And don't forget," he added, "I gave Giles half of Beaumont Center as part of your dowry."

Kate rolled her eyes in disgust. "I'm glad Elizabeth isn't hearing this. She'd box your ears."

Dismissing that with a wave of his hand he raced on. "All I have to do is figure out how to knock that chip off the boy's shoulder and get him to propose to Elizabeth."

Kate ran her tongue over her upper lip. "Ah...well, if it's a proposal you're hoping for, I don't expect you'll have long to wait. From what I heard on my way down here, I think negotiations are moving along nicely."

Teddy's expression went from shocked to delighted to indignant. "Good grief, girl, don't tell me you've taken up listening through keyholes?"

"Me?" Kate mimicked a ladylike sniff. "Really, Daddy. I'm a respectable, married woman. But...mmm...why don't we forget about that hot chocolate and have a brandy? I have a feeling a toast is in order."

Epilogue

Uncle Morgan! Not so close, you'll squish the baby."

Morgan drew Elizabeth's chair back a few inches from the table to allow for his wife's greatly expanded waistline and exchanged amused looks with her before leaning over to plant a kiss on the top of Rebecca's head. "Sorry, sweetheart. You're absolutely right. Junior's already complaining about the tight squeeze in there, as it is."

As he sat down, he thought it inconceivable how quickly time had slipped by. This time last year they had been sharing their first Thanksgiving together, elbow deep in plans for a January wedding. In the months that followed, Beaumont Center had opened to spectacular reviews, and in September Kate and Giles had celebrated the birth of their first child—a daughter they named Cassandra. Now Morgan and Elizabeth were about to become twofold parents.

As fate would have it, Rebecca had lost her mother in a car accident during an ice storm late in the winter. When Elizabeth came to him with the news that the child's father didn't want to take responsibility for her and to ask if they could adopt her he never hesitated. He knew how much the girl had come to mean to Elizabeth; it only compounded the deep feelings he already felt toward Rebecca himself. And very soon the second addition would arrive. A son, they'd discovered, after Elizabeth's doctor had recommended some tests.

Across the table, Kate sent her sister a smile of commiseration. "How's your back holding up? The last few weeks were killers for me. Giles was ready to hire a masseuse, because I wore him out, begging for back rubs."

"You forget I was veritably exhausted from driving all over creation, trying to keep you in those atrocious corn dog concoctions and caramel apples," Giles drawled beside her. He added a sly wink for Morgan. "If Cassie's teeth come through full of cavities, she has her mother's eating habits to thank."

At the head of the table Teddy leaned over to give a little push to the cradle that was placed between Kate and himself, and beamed at the tawny-haired infant blissfully sleeping inside. "She's going to have the teeth of a shark—just like her mother. Katy, remember how we had to replaster the wall in your room because you—"

"Daddy!" Kate cried as the others laughed. "How you carry on with those stories. Thank goodness, you didn't have a movie camera back then. I'd never be able to live down these tall tales."

"Did you really chew up the wall, Aunt Kate?" Rebecca asked, wide-eyed and giggly.

Kate shot her father another disgruntled look. "I'm afraid so. Your Aunt Liz was the civilized one in the family, always trying to dress me in layers of ruffles and lace like that Scarlett O'Hara doll she used to have. But," Kate added, eyeing the decorous picture the child made in her dark, ringlet curls and rose-colored velvet dress, "I have to admit you look pretty good all gussied up."

Laughing at Kate's choice of words as well as the way she wrinkled her nose, Rebecca leaned over to rest her head against Elizabeth's shoulder and lay her hand where she'd last felt the baby move. "Since I'm going to be her only daughter for a while, I thought I should let her have some fun. But as soon as this little guy is old enough, I'm getting back in my jeans and teaching him how to play baseball." After waiting for a minute, she turned, fixing Elizabeth with a worried stare. "I don't feel anything. I haven't felt him move since the other day."

Elizabeth smiled and stroked Rebecca's hair, not at all minding the question, just as she didn't mind that she rarely got a word in edgewise during these lively gatherings. It was enough that they were all together, healthy and happy, she thought, covering Rebecca's hand with her own. "He's resting," she explained patiently. "He's collecting his strength for his big moment." Feeling Morgan's light caress at her nape, she turned to find him watching her, and the look of absolute adoration in his eyes made her heart spill over with love.

They had so much to be grateful for this Thanksgiving. Admittedly it hadn't been the easiest year. Rebecca had been devastated when her mother was killed, and Morgan had had his hands full down at the stables. The plan to merge Meadowbrook and Wildwood was proving to be wonderfully successful, though because of the need to add on new stables, build a track, take down fences and seed new pastures, the actual purchase and breeding of thoroughbred racehorses wasn't going to get under way until next spring.

What had been most difficult was attaining a peace treaty between Spud and Jackson, whose clashing personalities had inspired counterproductivity and driven nearly everyone crazy. But a few months ago Spud had suffered a heart attack, and it had brought the cold war to a screeching halt. Jackson realized he was as deeply affected by the other man's illness as Morgan was and, as a result, an amusing, though dry-witted friendship was developing between the two crusty characters.

"Well, when are we going to eat?" Teddy grumbled, glaring at the kitchen door as if willing it to open. "Leona! People are starving out here."

"Dad, shh!" Elizabeth scolded softly. "You'll wake the baby."

"It would just give him an excuse to pick her up and spoil her some more," Leona announced, appearing through the swinging doors. In her hands was a huge platter, containing a golden-brown, roasted turkey. Everyone made appropriate sounds of appreciation and encouraged Teddy to hurry up and carve it.

"Wait—we have to make a toast first," he said, topping off another glass of wine and handing it to a startled Leona.

"Why, Mr. Beaumont…I don't know what to say."

"Hmph, now there's a first. Well, seeing as you've been around for almost as long as I have, I suppose it's time, don't you?" He raised his glass. However, when it came to making the toast, he found himself choked up. "Er, Morgan...son...why don't you do the honors?"

The appellation tightened Morgan's throat too, but as he felt Elizabeth take hold of his left hand, he picked up his glass with his right and stood.

"To family," he murmured gruffly.

"To family," everyone repeated.

After they all took a sip, the grown-ups of their wine and Rebecca and Elizabeth of their milk, everyone began passing dishes and giving Teddy requests for their favorite parts of the turkey. Morgan sat down, but before releasing Elizabeth's hand, he raised it to his lips for a tender kiss.

"And to love," he whispered, gazing deeply into her eyes.

Smiling through her tears, Elizabeth drew his hand to her stomach and leaned over to give him a gentle kiss. "To love."

* * * * *

Now appearing
in a special return engagement, Nora Roberts's
bestselling 1988 miniseries featuring

THE O'HURLEYS!
Nora Roberts

Book 1   **THE LAST HONEST WOMAN**   *Abby's Story*
Book 2   **DANCE TO THE PIPER**   *Maddy's Story*
Book 3   **SKIN DEEP**   *Chantel's Story*

And making his debut in a brand-new title, a very special
leading man ... Trace O'Hurley!

Book 4   **WITHOUT A TRACE**   *Trace's Tale*

In 1988, Nora Roberts introduced THE O'HURLEYS!—a close-knit
family of entertainers whose early travels spanned the country. The
beautiful triplet sisters and their mysterious brother each experience
the triumphant joy and passion only true love can bring, in four books
you will remember long after the last pages are turned.

Don't miss this captivating miniseries—a special collector's edition
available now wherever paperbacks are sold.

OHUR-1A

**From *New York Times* Bestselling author
Penny Jordan, a compelling novel of ruthless passion
that will mesmerize readers everywhere!**

Penny Jordan

Silver

Real power, true power came from
Rothwell. And Charles vowed to have it,
the earldom and all that went with it.

Silver vowed to destroy Charles, just as surely and
uncaringly as he had destroyed her father; just as he had
intended to destroy her. She needed him to want her . . .
to desire her . . . until he'd do anything to have her.

But first she needed a tutor: a man who wanted no one.
He would help her bait the trap.

**Played out on a glittering international stage,
Silver's story leads her from the luxurious comfort of
British aristocracy into the depths of adventure,
passion and danger.**

AVAILABLE NOW!

 HARLEQUIN

SIL-1A

Take 4 bestselling love stories FREE

Plus get a FREE surprise gift!

Double your reading pleasure this fall with two Award of Excellence titles written by two of your favorite authors.

Available in September

DUNCAN'S BRIDE
by Linda Howard
Silhouette Intimate Moments #349

Mail-order bride Madelyn Patterson was nothing like what Reese Duncan expected—and everything he needed.

Available in October

THE COWBOY'S LADY
by Debbie Macomber
Silhouette Special Edition #626

The Montana cowboy wanted a little lady at his beck and call—the ''lady'' in question saw things differently....

These titles have been selected to receive a special laurel—the Award of Excellence. Look for the distinctive emblem on the cover. It lets you know there's something truly wonderful inside!

DUN-1

Win 1 of 10 Romantic Vacations and Earn Valuable Travel Coupons Worth up to $1,000!

Inside every Harlequin or Silhouette book during September, October and November, you will find a PASSPORT TO ROMANCE that could take you around the world.

By sending us the official entry form available at your favorite retail store, you will automatically be entered in the PASSPORT TO ROMANCE sweepstakes, which could win you a star-studded London Show Tour, a Carribean Cruise, a fabulous tour of France, a sun-drenched visit to Hawaii, a Mediterranean Cruise or a wander through Britain's historical castles. The more entry forms you send in, the better your chances of winning!

In addition to your chances of winning a fabulous vacation for two, valuable travel discounts on hotels, cruises, car rentals and restaurants can be yours by submitting an offer certificate (available at retail stores) properly completed with proofs-of-purchase from any specially marked PASSPORT TO ROMANCE Harlequin® or Silhouette® book. The more proofs-of-purchase you collect, the higher the value of travel coupons received!

For details on your PASSPORT TO ROMANCE, look for information at your favorite retail store or send a self-addressed stamped envelope to:

PASSPORT TO ROMANCE
P.O. Box 621
Fort Erie, Ontario L2A 5X3

ONE PROOF-OF-PURCHASE

3-CSD-2

To collect your free coupon booklet you must include the necessary number of proofs-of-purchase with a properly completed offer certificate available in retail stores or from the above address.